Blood Money

A Psychological Thriller of Survival, Power, and Revenge

Howard Kane

Hidden Alpha Capital LLC

About the author

Howard Kane writes the stories most people are afraid to tell.

As a former Fortune 500 executive, he knows what it feels like to appear successful on the outside while quietly unraveling on the inside. For years, he hid his drinking behind late nights, busy calendars, and a polished smile. When he finally faced the truth about his addiction, he discovered that recovery wasn't just possible; it was life-changing.

Howard channels that experience into memoir-style novels that explore addiction, family trauma, money, and power. His five-book saga, ***The Daughter of a Drunk***, follows Olivia Parker from a terrified little girl in a small Ohio town, vowing she'll never be like her father, to a woman fighting billionaires, corrupt institutions, and her own worst impulses. The series blends coming-of-age drama, generational alcoholism, and high-stakes whistleblower suspense into one continuous, bingeable story.

He also writes standalone novels rooted in alcohol dependence and recovery, including ***The Double Life of a High-Functioning Alcoholic***, which pulls back the curtain on the addiction that hides behind ambition and success, and ***From Wine Mom to Sober Mom***, which shines a light on the unique struggles mothers face when drinking threatens everything they love.

Through raw honesty and lived experience, Howard's books show that surviving a drunk parent or being the drunk parent is only the beginning. The real story is what you do with the wreckage. Readers describe his work as "impossible to put down" because the characters feel uncomfortably real, and their choices never come cheap.

If you've ever questioned your relationship with drinking, grown up in the shadow of someone else's, or wondered how far you'd go to protect the people you love, Howard Kane's stories are for you.

Website: https://selfcarejourneybooks.com/

Contents

Chapter One

The Name

I'M FLOATING.

Not falling. Floating. Somewhere near the ceiling of a room with no windows. Just black walls and that pine smell. Chemical-sweet, covering something rotten.

Below me, there's a body on the bed. It takes too long to realize it's mine.

My wrists are tied. Silk. The kind that doesn't leave marks. My arms lie at wrong angles, as if someone arranged a doll and walked away.

My mouth is open. Making sounds.

"Please. Please. Please."

But I'm not down there saying it. I'm up here. Trapped. Watching myself beg.

Move. I scream at my body. *Get up. Fight.*

Nothing happens.

The drug cut every wire. I can see everything, feel everything, understand everything. But I can't make my fingers twitch. Can't make my legs work. Can't do anything but witness.

He's smoothing his white shirt. Again.

Palms flat against the linen. Checking the creases. Making sure everything is perfect.

"You're fighting it," he says. Too calm. Clinical. "That's normal. They always fight at first. But they stop soon."

The Bach gets louder. Violins screaming things I can't scream.

I try to dive back into my body. Force my way in. Reclaim what's mine. But there's nothing to grab onto. I'm a ghost haunting my own assault.

My head turns below. Slow. Wrong. My eyes are open. I can see from two places at once: from the ceiling and from inside that useless body.

He's looking at me with empty eyes. Doll's eyes. Something pretending to be human. He smooths his shirt.

My body whispers something. Barely audible under the music.

He tilts his head. "Forty-seven times you've said please tonight. I've been counting."

The pine smell is choking me. But I don't have lungs up here. Don't have a throat. Just awareness. Just this terrible watching.

He unbuttons his cuff. Checks the alignment. Buttons it again.

"Mother taught me that presentation builds trust. People see what they expect to see."

Another smooth of the white shirt. Ritual. Steps he follows each time.

"I prefer my companions compliant."

Please. My body begs below. Tiny. Broken. Nobody hears me. I try again to get back in. To reconnect. To be whole.

He crouches closer. Face inches from mine.

"You've already consumed a significant dose," he whispers. "Best to let it take its course. Fighting creates complications."

His hand moves. My body flinches or tries to. The movement is sluggish. And I realize with crystal clarity: this will never end. I'll be here forever. Trapped above myself. Watching him destroy me while I can't lift a finger to stop it.

My body is making sounds again. Not words anymore. Just animal noises.

"Do you know how easy it was?" He's circling now. Slow steps. "Clean khakis and a white shirt. Suddenly, homeless prostitutes think I'm safe."

The Bach builds toward something terrible. His laugh echoes. "That's just the mammal brain's last stand before the medication finishes its work."

And I'm still floating. Still watching. Still screaming with no voice while the drug keeps me split in two. Consciousness sharp as a knife and body dead as meat.

The ritual smoothing. The empty eyes. The pine smell. Forever.

"Olivia!"

Linda's voice crashed through the memory. Real. Present. Desperate.

"Baby, wake up! You're safe. You're home."

I gasped. My eyes flew open. Not the penthouse. Not the darkness.

Linda's guest room. February morning light. Millfield.

Four months since that night. Four months pregnant. Four months of waking up drowning.

My hands flew to my throat, checking for fingerprints that had faded weeks ago but still burned. The silk around my wrists. The paralysis. I could still feel all of it carved into my bones.

"You're in Millfield," Linda said, her hands warm on my shoulders. Anchoring me. "You're safe."

Safe. The word was a lie we both pretended to believe.

My heart slammed against my ribs. Sweat soaked through my nightshirt. The sheets were twisted around my legs. Like restraints. I kicked them off and scrambled out of bed. My hands shook so badly I had to grip the dresser.

For a second, the room tilted and I was back there, watching my body make sounds I couldn't control while he studied me like I was data and the violins played mathematical perfection.

"I'm okay," I lied. "I'm fine."

Linda didn't argue. We both knew better.

"I'll make coffee," she said softly. "Decaf for you."

She left me alone in the room that used to be mine. Before college. Before McKinsey. Before I became someone who woke up on penthouse floors with hours cut out of her life.

I sat on the bed, hands on my stomach where the baby, Grace (I'd already named her Grace) was growing. Four months along.

My whole body screamed for vodka. The only thing that could make the nightmares stop. The only thing that could quiet the memories. The drugged wine, the floating sensation, the watching myself disappear while Bach played and I couldn't get back in.

The bottle was in Linda's shed. Dad's old stash. Just sitting there behind the rakes, dusty and full, waiting. I hadn't touched it yet.

But God, I wanted to.

Because when I was drunk, I couldn't see those empty eyes or hear myself begging or feel the silk cutting into my wrists or smell the expensive cologne.

Day 122 of sobriety meant feeling all of it. Every second. No escape.

Grace kicked again. Harder. Like she knew what I was thinking. This baby I'd poisoned for six weeks with vodka. This baby conceived in violence who kept fighting anyway.

I got dressed slowly. Maternity jeans from Goodwill. A sweater that smelled like fabric softener and safety. I walked downstairs on legs that felt unsteady.

The kitchen smelled like coffee and toast. Normal things. Things that felt impossible.

"Eat," Linda said, sliding a plate across the table.

I stared at the eggs. My stomach turned.

"Detective Smith called again," Linda said carefully. "Fourth time this week."

My hands froze on the fork.

The DNA results. The name of the man who'd drugged me, tied me down, and counted my begging like I was an experiment.

But I already knew his face. I saw it every time I closed my eyes.

"I can't," I whispered.

"You don't have to—"

"I can't do this." My voice cracked. "Can't stay sober. Can't raise this baby. Can't live with what happened to me. My body won't let me forget."

Tears streamed down my face. Hot. Endless.

Linda pulled me into her arms.

"I know, baby. I know."

"And I'm carrying his baby. A piece of the worst night of my life growing inside me, and I should hate her, but—"

Grace kicked again.

"But she's fighting," I whispered.

Linda squeezed my shoulders. "So fight with her."

"I don't know how."

"Yes, you do. You're doing it right now. Every day you stay sober. Every time you choose to stay here instead of disappearing into the vodka."

I pulled back and looked at her through tears.

"I'll call Detective Smith," I said finally. "I'll find out the name. I'll face it."

Because Grace was fighting, despite being conceived in violence and being poisoned. Despite having a mother who spent four months floating above her own body in nightmares.

If she could fight, maybe I could too. Even if every breath felt like dying.

I picked up the phone and dialed before I could think about the bottle. Before I could think about the wine glass heavy in my hand, the room spinning, and his voice saying, *"I prefer my companions compliant"* while the drug stole everything.

The phone rang.

"Ms. Parker?" Detective Smith's voice came through the phone. Professional. Careful. "Thank you for calling me back."

I sat at Linda's kitchen table. Four months sober. One hundred twenty-two days.

And I was about to find out who had raped me. Who had fathered Grace.

"I'm here," I said.

"Can you come to the station? I think this is a conversation we should have in person."

Linda squeezed my shoulder, steadying me.

"Okay," I whispered. "I'll be there in an hour."

I stood up, grabbed my jacket, and let Linda drive me to the police station. And I tried not to think about what I'd do after I learned his name.

The detective's office smelled like burned coffee and old files. I'd been in this room four times now, telling the same story to different people who looked at me with the same expression, as if I were a problem they didn't know how to solve.

Four months pregnant. Sitting in a chair that creaked every time I shifted my weight. Grace moved inside me like a question I couldn't answer.

Detective Smith looked tired. Not the kind of tired that comes from one bad night, but the kind that builds up over years of hearing stories like mine.

"Ms. Parker, I want to be straight with you." He pushed a folder across the table. "We got the DNA results back from your rape kit."

My hands went to my stomach automatically.

"And?"

"The DNA matches Tyler Carrington."

The name hit me like cold water.

Tyler. The man in the penthouse with the marble bathroom and Bach playing softly while he tied my wrists. The one who'd smiled when he handed me wine that tasted wrong. Who'd raped me while I couldn't move, couldn't scream, couldn't do anything but float somewhere above my own body, watching it happen.

He had a name now. A real name, not just "him," "the man," or "that night I try not to remember."

"Do you know who his mother is?" Detective Smith asked gently.

I shook my head, but something cold was already crawling up my spine.

"Margaret Carrington. CEO of Carrington Media."

The name hit me like a fist to the stomach.

Margaret Carrington.

The Peninsula Hotel. The night I'd lost everything. I had been trying to land the Carrington account: $2 million, which was supposed to be my ticket to promotion. I'd watched her husband David and his colleagues mock homeless people, imitate "twitching junkies," and make zombie faces while they laughed about attempted robberies.

That was the night I'd screamed about Leo in front of three hundred people. The night the viral video started. The night Margaret Carrington had watched me collapse on the marble floor while security carried me away.

And then, months later, she'd walked into Nordstrom and recognized me folding clothes for twelve dollars an hour. She savored every second of my humiliation while trying on dresses and asking about my "family" with fake concern dripping from every word.

Then, she made a phone call. Thirty seconds of conversation. And I was fired.

Margaret Carrington had systematically destroyed what was left of my life. And now—

"No," I whispered. "No, no, no."

Detective Smith's expression showed he didn't understand. "Ms. Parker?"

"His mother is Margaret Carrington?" My voice came out strangled. "The Margaret Carrington?"

"You know her?"

"She—" I struggled to catch my breath. I looked up at Detective Smith. "She's already destroyed my life once. And now her son—"

I couldn't finish the sentence.

Her son had raped me. He had tied me down, drugged me, and left me cold on his bathroom floor. And she had billions of dollars and an army of lawyers, and she'd already proven she could obliterate me with a single phone call.

"This is why you don't think you can prosecute," I said. "Because it's her. Because she owns half of Chicago."

Detective Smith's silence was answer enough.

"It's a large media company," he said quietly. "Publishing, digital media, content creation. Worth about ten billion dollars. And Ms. Carrington has... resources. Unlimited resources."

The room tilted. I gripped the edge of the table.

"So what happens now?" My voice came out smaller than I intended.

Detective Smith leaned back in his chair. It creaked. Everything in this building creaked. The floors, the chairs, and the futures of girls like me.

"I believe you, Olivia. The evidence supports your account. But I need you to understand what you're up against."

"Money."

"Yes, you are right. Money. Power. Lawyers who went to Harvard and Yale. PR firms that can make you look like the villain in your own assault." He paused.

"Can we still prosecute?"

Detective Smith's face told me the answer before he said it.

"The DA's office is reviewing the case. But between you and me? They're not optimistic. Carrington's legal team is already filing motions. Character assassination. Reasonable doubt. They'll argue consent, that you were working, that this was a transaction you regretted later."

"He drugged me."

"I know. But the only substance in your system was alcohol. You'd been drinking before you met him. You told us that yourself. His lawyers will say you drank too much, blacked out, and invented the drugging to justify feelings of guilt about the encounter."

The encounter. Like rape was just something that happened to me, not something he did.

"So he gets away with it."

"I'm sorry. I really am." Detective Smith looked like he meant it. "We'll keep investigating. Sometimes new evidence surfaces. Other victims come forward. But you should prepare yourself for the reality that this case might not go anywhere."

I stood up. My legs felt like water, but I made them hold me.

"Thank you for believing me."

"Of course I believe you. I just wish belief was enough."

Linda was waiting in the car outside the police station. She'd driven me here, taken off work at the diner to sit with me through this. Her face was tight with worry.

"What did they say?"

"His name is Tyler Carrington. His mother runs Carrington Media."

Linda went pale. Even she'd heard of Carrington Media. Everyone had.

"Oh, baby."

"They don't think they can prosecute. Too much money. Too many lawyers." I stared out the window at the parking lot. "I was raped by a billionaire's son, and nobody's going to do anything about it."

Linda's hand found mine. Her palm was rough from years of carrying hot plates and wiping down tables. It felt like the only real thing in the world.

"Then we figure out what comes next."

"What if there is no next? What if this is it? He wins, I lose, and Grace grows up knowing her father is a rapist who got away with it?"

"Then you survive anyway. Like you've been surviving. One day at a time."

I wanted to believe her. But how easy it would be to just stop fighting. Stop choosing sobriety. Stop pretending I was strong enough for this.

We drove home in silence. Home. That's what Linda's house was now. The same house where I'd grown up hiding from Dad's rages. The same house I'd sworn I'd never return to.

But here I was. Pregnant. Broken. Starting over in the place I'd spent my whole life trying to escape.

The legal aid lawyer's office was in a strip mall between a nail salon and a discount shoe store. Her name was Patricia Clarkson, and she looked about twelve years old.

"I've reviewed your case," she said, shuffling papers on a desk held together with duct tape. "The evidence is strong. The rape kit, the medical records, your consistent statements. In a fair world, you'd win."

"But we don't live in a fair world."

"No. We don't." She looked at me with tired eyes that belonged to someone much older. "Carrington has unlimited resources. They can drag this out for years. Appeals, motions, delays. They'll file so much paperwork you'll drown in it. And they'll destroy your character in the process."

"So what do I do?"

"You have three options. One fight. Spend years in court, endure the publicity, and probably lose anyway. Two: take a settlement if they offer one. Sign an NDA, take the money, and never speak about it again. Three: walk away. No money, no justice, but also no more trauma."

I pressed my hands against my stomach. Grace kicked, tiny thumps against my palm like Morse code. Like she was trying to tell me something.

"I can't walk away. And I can't sign away my right to tell the truth."

"Then you're looking at option one. And I have to be honest. It will destroy you. The media coverage, the scrutiny, the lawyers tearing apart every choice you've ever made. You're four months sober. Can you stay sober through years of that?"

The question hung in the air between us.

Could I?

I thought about the vodka bottle in the shed, how my hands shook every morning, and how I still woke up at 3 AM with my heart pounding, tasting wine that shouldn't be there.

"I don't know," I whispered.

Patricia's face softened. "That's honest. And honestly? I'd advise you to consider all your options carefully, not because you don't deserve justice, but because pursuing it might cost you everything you have left."

Chapter Two

Above the Law

THEY CAME ON A Thursday afternoon.

I was in Linda's kitchen making tea when I heard the car. Not just any car. The kind that costs more than Linda's house. A black Mercedes SUV with tinted windows pulled up to the curb like it owned the whole street.

My stomach dropped before I even saw who got out.

Two men in dark suits emerged first. Bodyguards. They moved like professionals, scanning the neighborhood as if Linda's quiet street in Millfield were enemy territory. One stayed by the car, hand resting inside his jacket. The other walked the perimeter of Linda's yard, eyes moving constantly.

And then she stepped out.

Margaret Carrington.

She wore a cream-colored Chanel suit that probably cost what Linda made in six months. Her silver hair was styled perfectly, not a strand out of place. Diamond earrings caught the afternoon sun. She moved with the kind of confidence that comes from never worrying about money in your entire life.

Even standing on a cracked sidewalk in front of a house with peeling paint and an overgrown lawn.

I watched through the window as she looked at Linda's house. Really looked at it. Her nose wrinkled slightly, like she'd caught a whiff of something unpleasant. Her eyes swept over the rusted mailbox, the sagging porch, the neighbors' yard full of broken toys, and an above-ground pool with a hole in it.

She was cataloging our poverty. Filing it away like evidence in a case she was building.

This was the woman who'd watched me shatter at the Peninsula Hotel. Who'd seen me fold clothes at Nordstrom and savored every second of my humiliation. Who'd made one phone call and destroyed what little I had left.

And now she was here. On Linda's lawn. About to walk into the house where I'd grown up.

Linda came up behind me. "Who is that?"

"Margaret Carrington." My voice came out flat. Dead.

"Tyler's mother?"

"Yeah."

"What does she want?"

The doorbell rang. The bodyguard on the porch stood with his back to the door, scanning the street as if assassins might leap from behind the overgrown hedges.

Linda opened the door. I stood behind her, hands on my swollen belly, feeling Grace kick against my palms like she could sense the danger.

Margaret's face broke into a smile that didn't reach her eyes.

"Good to see you again, Olivia."

Her voice was smooth. Pleasant. Like we were old friends running into each other at the country club instead of a rapist's mother and a rape victim meeting.

"Mrs. Carrington," Linda said, her voice cold. "What do you want?"

Margaret's smile tightened just slightly. "You must be Olivia's mother. Linda, is it?"

She said Linda's name like she was testing out a foreign word. Something unfamiliar and slightly distasteful.

"I'm here to speak with Olivia." Margaret's eyes flicked past Linda to me. "About a matter of some urgency."

"Anything you have to say, you can say in front of my mother," I said.

Margaret's gaze moved slowly over me. Taking in my swollen belly, my bare feet, my unwashed hair pulled back in a ponytail. I watched her catalog every detail of my decline, just like she'd done at Nordstrom. But this time, there was something else in her eyes.

Satisfaction.

"Very well," she said. "May I come in?"

"No." Linda's voice was steel.

For just a second, Margaret looked genuinely surprised. Like she wasn't used to hearing that word. She probably wasn't. People like her didn't get told no.

"I see." Her smile never wavered. "Then I'll be brief." She glanced at the neighbors' houses, at the cars driving past. "Though I imagine you'd prefer to have this conversation privately. It concerns a rather... delicate matter."

She let the word hang there. Delicate. Like my rape was something embarrassing we should discuss behind closed doors.

"We're fine here," Linda said.

Margaret's eyes hardened. Just for a second. Then the smile was back.

"As you wish." She reached into her designer handbag. Hermes. I recognized it from my McKinsey days. She pulled out an envelope. Thick, expensive paper. "I'm here to make you an offer, Olivia. A generous one, considering the circumstances."

"I don't want your money."

"You haven't heard the terms yet." Margaret held up one perfectly manicured hand. "Two hundred thousand dollars. That's more than enough to get you back on your feet. Find an apartment. Provide for that child." Her eyes dropped to my stomach again. "Give her opportunities."

Her. She already knew the baby was a girl. Of course she did. She probably had investigators digging through every aspect of my life.

"In exchange," Margaret continued, her voice businesslike now, clinical, "you sign a non-disclosure agreement. You never speak publicly about this alleged incident with my son. You never contact him. You never make any claims of paternity or child support."

The words landed like slaps.

Alleged incident. Attempting to manufacture. Like I'd invented the rape. Like Grace wasn't a baby but a scheme.

"There's also a document relinquishing any future claims to the Carrington estate," Margaret said, pulling more papers from her bag. "You sign away any right to inheritance, financial support, or any association with our family name. Forever."

She held out the envelope like she was offering me a life raft.

"This is quite generous, really. Two hundred thousand dollars is more money than someone in your position will ever see otherwise." Her eyes swept over Linda's house again. Over the peeling paint, the cracked windows, the poverty we couldn't hide. "I imagine it's more than you've had in your entire life combined."

Linda's hand tightened on my arm. Warning me. But my whole body was shaking.

"You think I got pregnant on purpose?" The words came out hoarse. "You think I wanted this?"

Margaret tilted her head, studying me like I was a specimen under glass.

"I think you saw an opportunity." Her tone was matter-of-fact. Like she was stating an obvious truth to a child. "A wealthy young man. A single encounter. A pregnancy that could potentially be tied to our family." She paused. "It's not uncommon for women in desperate situations to manufacture these kinds of connections."

"HE RAPED ME!"

The words exploded out of me. Loud enough that the bodyguard on the porch shifted, hand moving inside his jacket.

Margaret didn't even blink.

"That's your allegation, yes." She said it the way you'd say "you claim the sky is green." Polite disagreement with something obviously false. "Which the police seem disinclined to pursue. I wonder why that is?"

She knew exactly why. She'd made sure of it.

"Perhaps," Margaret continued, her voice dripping with false sympathy, "it's because your history makes you s omewhat... less than credible. The viral video from the Peninsula. The prostitution charges. The substance abuse issues." She ticked them off on her fingers like items on a shopping list. "Even I felt sorry for you when I saw you at Nordstrom. You looked so lost."

There it was. The reminder that she'd seen me at my lowest. That she'd watched me fall and enjoyed every second.

"My son made a mistake engaging with someone of your... background." Margaret's nose wrinkled slightly, like the word itself smelled bad.

"But that doesn't entitle you to destroy his life. Or mine. Or to use that child..." She gestured at my stomach with barely disguised disgust. "...as leverage to extract money from my family."

"Get off my property." Linda's voice cut through the air like a blade.

Margaret ignored her. Kept her eyes locked on mine. Those cold, calculating eyes that had cataloged my destruction at Nordstrom. That had watched me sob on marble floors at the Peninsula.

"Let me be very clear, Olivia." She took a step closer. Close enough that I could smell her perfume. Expensive. Suffocating. "You will never win a case against my son. The DA knows it. That bargain-basement lawyer of yours knows it. And deep down, you know it too."

Her smile was razor-thin.

"I have resources you cannot begin to imagine. Lawyers who will dissect every choice you've ever made. Investigators who will find every ugly secret you're hiding. Media outlets that will publish whatever story serves my interests."

She leaned in closer.

"I destroyed your career at McKinsey with a single phone call. Got you fired from Nordstrom just as easily. And that was when I wasn't even trying. Imagine what I can do when I'm actually motivated."

My hands were fists now. Nails digging into my palms so hard I felt blood.

"This offer—" Margaret held up the envelope again. "—is the only sensible choice. You're not taking it because you're smart. You're taking it because fighting me will break you completely. That baby will grow up watching her mother lose everything while I make absolutely certain you can never work, never recover, never have a single moment of peace."

She smiled. "I'll make sure that when people Google your name, all they see is a cautionary tale. A reminder of what happens when someone from your station tries to reach above their place."

The words hung in the air like poison.

This was who Margaret Carrington really was. Not the polished CEO in business magazines. Not the philanthropist at charity galas. This was the woman who believed some people were simply better than others. That money and power meant you could destroy whoever you wanted.

And she was Tyler's mother. She'd raised him to believe the same thing: that people like me were disposable, usable, things to be discarded when you were done.

"Sign the papers," Margaret said. "Take the money. Disappear. It's the only choice that doesn't end with you completely destroyed."

Something inside me cracked. Not broke. Cracked. Like ice on a frozen lake. And underneath was fire.

"Get. Out."

Margaret raised an eyebrow. "Excuse me?"

"You heard me." I stepped forward, putting myself between her and my mother. Between her and my home. "Get out of our house. Get off our property. And tell your rapist son that he can go to hell."

"Miss Parker—"

"No." My voice was shaking, but it was loud. Strong. "You don't get to come here and treat me like garbage. You don't get to look at my mother's home—" My voice broke. "—like it's disgusting. Like we're beneath you. You don't get to call my daughter a scheme."

Tears streamed down my face, but I didn't care.

"Your son drugged me. He tied me down. He raped me while I couldn't move or scream or fight back. And you th ink... you actually think... that I would want anything from him? From you? That I want your blood money?"

Margaret's expression finally changed. Not shame. Not guilt. Not even anger.

Annoyance. Like I was a child throwing a tantrum. Like I was being difficult and making her day harder than it needed to be.

"You're making a mistake," she said.

"No. You made the mistake." I stepped closer, close enough to see my own reflection in her cold eyes. "Coming here. Threatening me. Thinking you can buy my silence."

I grabbed the envelope from her hand and ripped it in half. Then in half again. The papers fluttered to the porch like snow.

"I will never take your money. I will never sign your papers. And I will never, ever let you erase what your son did to me."

My voice dropped. Got quieter. More dangerous.

"I will pay you back for this. For all of it. Every humiliation. Every threat. Everything you've done to me and my family. For the Peninsula. For Nordstrom. For coming here and treating us like we're nothing."

For the first time, Margaret actually looked at me. Really looked. Not through me. Not past me. At me.

And then she laughed. It started as a chuckle and built into a full, genuine laugh. The kind that made her bodyguards shift uncomfortably. The kind that echoed across Linda's quiet street.

"You?" She wiped her eyes as if I'd told the funniest joke she'd heard all year. "You're going to make me pay?"

She laughed again, shaking her head. Her perfect hair didn't move.

"Oh, sweetheart." The condescension in her voice was thick enough to choke on. "You're a homeless drunk with a prostitution record and a baby you can't afford. You couldn't hurt me if you tried."

She leaned in close. Her smile was venomous.

"You couldn't even keep a twelve-dollar-an-hour job after I made one phone call. And you think you can touch me? Touch my company? My family?"

Her eyes glittered with something dark.

"You will never be able to do anything to me or my son. Never. I will make absolutely certain of it." She straightened, adjusting her perfect suit. "I will make sure you never get work again. Any job you apply for, any opportunity that might open for you. I'll close it. I will ensure that every door that could possibly open for you stays locked."

She stepped closer, invading my space.

"I will make sure that when people Google your name, when they see your face, all they see is a cautionary tale. A warning about what happens to women who aim above their station. Who try to trap wealthy men with pregnancy scams. Who lie about rape for money."

Her smile widened.

"By the time I'm done, you won't be able to get a job cleaning toilets. Your daughter will grow up knowing her mother is a joke. A failure. A liar who destroyed her own life."

She paused, making sure I felt every word.

"You want to fight me? Go ahead. I'll enjoy watching you drown. I'll enjoy watching you lose custody of that child when you can't provide for her. When the courts see you're unstable, unemployed, unemployable."

Margaret turned to leave, then paused at the steps.

"The offer expires in forty-eight hours. After that, you get nothing but the misery you're choosing." Her eyes swept over me one last time. "Enjoy your poverty, Olivia. You've earned it."

Then, she was gone. The bodyguards followed. The Mercedes pulled away slowly, deliberately, leaving deep tire tracks in Linda's lawn like a final insult.

I stood there, staring at the torn papers scattered across the porch. Two hundred thousand dollars, ripped into pieces.

Linda put her arms around me. I collapsed into her, sobbing so hard I couldn't breathe.

"I can't beat her," I choked out. "She's right. I can't do anything. I'm nobody."

"Hey." Linda pulled back, grabbed my face in her hands. "You listen to me. You are not nobody. You are my daughter. You are Grace's mother. And you just told one of the most powerful women in America to go to hell."

"And she laughed at me."

"Let her laugh." Linda's eyes were fierce. "Let her think she's won. Because she doesn't know you, baby. She doesn't know what you're made of."

Linda's grip tightened.

"She doesn't know that you survived your father. Survived Leo's death. Survived the streets. She thinks money is power. She thinks she can break you because she broke you before."

"She's right, though. I'm nothing. I have nothing."

"You have something she'll never have." Linda's voice was steel. "You have the truth. And you have the will to fight even when you're terrified. Even when you have every reason to give up."

"What if I lose?"

"Then you lose fighting. But at least you'll lose on your feet, not on your knees signing her papers."

That night, I went back out to the shed.

I stood there looking at the vodka bottle in the dusty light from the single bulb hanging overhead.

Four months sober. The longest stretch since Leo died. The longest stretch since the night I found him in that morgue with his hands folded across his chest like he was sleeping.

Margaret Carrington's words kept looping in my head. *You're a homeless drunk with a prostitution record. You couldn't hurt me if you tried.*

She was right. That's exactly what I was.

I picked up the bottle. Felt the weight of it. Unscrewed the cap.

The smell hit me immediately. Sharp, clean, and promising. One drink to make the pain stop. Just one drink to quiet the screaming in my head that said I was stupid for turning down two hundred thousand dollars, stupid for thinking I could fight a billionaire, stupid for believing anyone would ever believe me over Tyler Carrington.

I lifted it to my lips. And then I heard Leo's voice. Not real. I knew it wasn't real. But I heard it anyway.

"You don't want to do that, Livvy."

I looked up. He was standing in the corner of the shed where the shadows were deepest. Young and whole, the way he'd been before the drugs. Before the hollow eyes and shaking hands.

"It didn't help me," he said quietly. "It won't help you either."

"I can't do this." My voice broke. "I can't stay sober through this. It's too hard."

"Then don't stay sober through this. Just stay sober right now. This minute. That's all you have to do."

"And then what? The next minute? And the minute after that? Forever?"

"No. Just now. Just this moment. You can do anything for one moment."

I stood there holding that bottle.

"I miss you," I whispered. "I miss you so much, and I'm so sorry I didn't save you."

"I know. But you can save her." He looked at my stomach, where Grace was growing. "You can break the cycle. For both of us."

"Margaret's right, though. I can't beat her. I'm nothing."

"Dad thought that too. Thought he was nothing. Drank because of it." Leo's eyes were sad. "But you're not nothing, Livvy. You never were. You just believed the wrong people when they told you who you are."

When I looked up again, he was gone. Just shadows and dust and the smell of vodka that I was still holding like a loaded gun.

I walked back to the house. Poured the vodka down the kitchen sink while Linda watched from the doorway.

"Good choice," she said quietly.

"I almost didn't make it."

"But you did. That's what counts."

I rinsed the bottle. Threw it in the recycling. Went to my room and lay on the bed with my hands on my stomach.

"I'm trying, Grace," I whispered. "I'm trying so hard. I hope someday you'll know that."

The baby kicked again. One small thump. Like she was answering. Like she believed me.

Three weeks later, the prosecutor called me in.

Her name was Dana Whitaker, and she looked like she'd been fighting this same battle for twenty years. Tired eyes behind wire-rimmed glasses. Gray roots showing through brown hair that needed a trim. A coffee stain on her blouse that she'd tried to cover with a blazer.

She was the kind of prosecutor who believed in justice but had learned the hard way that believing wasn't enough.

We sat in a windowless conference room that smelled like stale coffee and broken promises. The table was scarred with years of other people's tragedies. I wondered how many women had sat in this exact chair, waiting to hear if their rapist would face consequences.

"I've reviewed your case thoroughly," Dana said. She had a file open in front of her. My life reduced to paper. "The evidence supports your account. The medical examination. The rape kit. Detective Smith's notes. Your consistent statements."

Hope flickered in my chest. Fragile. Desperate.

"I believe you were raped, Olivia."

The words hung in the air for a moment. Someone believed me. A prosecutor with twenty years of experience looked at my case and believed me.

"But—"

The match went out.

"But I can't file charges."

The room tilted. I gripped the edge of the table.

"Why not?"

Dana took off her glasses, rubbed her eyes, and put them back on as if she needed the armor.

"Insufficient likelihood of conviction. That's the official language. What it means is: I believe you, but a jury probably won't. Or if they do believe you, they won't convict."

She opened a different folder, this one much thicker.

"Tyler Carrington's legal team filed their first motions before we even had the DNA results back. Fifty-three pages. They have six lawyers on retainer. Six. For a case we haven't even charged yet."

Dana spread some papers across the table. Motions. Legal briefs. All with the letterhead of Sterling & Katz, one of the most expensive law firms in the country.

"They're arguing consent. They'll say you went to his apartment voluntarily. That you're a sex worker who regretted a transaction. That your history of prostitution and substance abuse makes you an unreliable witness."

Each word was a knife.

"They'll put your entire life on trial, Olivia. Every choice you've made. Every moment you were desperate. They'll take your worst days and hold them up as proof that you're a liar."

"But the rape kit—"

"Shows trauma consistent with forcible rape. But it doesn't prove lack of consent. Not to a jury. Not when the defense will argue that sex work often involves rough encounters."

I tasted bile.

"The drug test came back clean except for alcohol. You told the hospital you'd been drinking before you met him. His lawyers will say you drank too much, blacked out, and invented the drugging story to justify regret."

"I didn't invent it." My voice was barely a whisper.

"I know. But proving what you remember versus what you don't remember versus what actually happened? In front of a jury? When you admit there are hours you can't account for?" Dana shook her head. "His lawyers will destroy you with that."

She pulled out another document. This one had photos attached.

I saw myself. Multiple versions of myself. Getting arrested for prostitution, stumbling drunk outside a bar, the viral video from the Peninsula Hotel where I had an emotional breakdown in front of hundreds of people.

"Where did they get those?"

"Public record. Social media. Private investigators. The Carrington family has resources we can't begin to match." Dana's voice was gentle but firm. "And this is just what they filed in preliminary motions. Imagine what they'll do at actual trial."

She leaned forward.

"I've been doing this for twenty-three years. I've seen women with perfect lives, pristine reputations, and ironclad evidence fail to get convictions in rape cases. The system is broken. You know it. I know it."

"So he just gets away with it."

"I didn't say that." Dana's eyes softened. "I said I can't file charges with a reasonable likelihood of conviction. That's the standard I have to meet. But that doesn't mean you're without options."

"What options?"

"Civil suit. Lower burden of proof. You could potentially win damages."

"With what lawyer? I'm living in my mother's guest room, and I have three hundred dollars to my name."

Dana nodded like she'd expected that answer.

"Then you wait. Sometimes other victims come forward. Sometimes new evidence surfaces. Sometimes the statute of limitations becomes your friend because these men... they don't stop. They can't help themselves."

The words settled over me like ash.

Tyler Carrington would rape again. And maybe then... maybe when there were multiple victims, multiple stories, multiple women brave enough to come forward... maybe then someone would stop him.

But not now. Not for me.

"I'm sorry, Olivia." Dana closed the folders. "I really am. This isn't justice. But it's the reality we're working with."

I stood up. My legs felt like water, but I made them hold me.

"Thank you for believing me."

"Of course I believe you." Dana stood too. "I just wish belief was enough."

I went home and sat in Linda's bathroom.

The same bathroom where, at six years old, I'd made a promise to God that I'd never be like my father. That I'd never drink, never hurt people, never make my children scared.

The tiles were the same pale yellow they'd been for thirty years. Linda scrubbed the grout every weekend with a toothbrush, but it never got completely clean. Brown stains in the cracks. Proof that some dirt goes too deep to reach.

The mirror had a crack running from the upper right corner down toward the center. A spiderweb of damage from when Dad threw a beer bottle seventeen years ago. Linda could have replaced it. Should have replaced it. But she never did.

Maybe she needed the reminder. Maybe we both did.

I sat on the closed toilet lid, knees pulled up to my chest as much as my swollen belly would allow. Grace kicked against my ribs, protesting the cramped space, telling me to sit up straight.

I pulled out my phone. Looked at my reflection in the black screen before I turned it on. Hollow cheeks. Dark circles. Hair that hadn't been washed in three days pulled back in a greasy ponytail.

This was the face that would tell my daughter's truth.

I hit record.

For a long moment, I just stared at the camera. At my own face staring back. What was I supposed to say? How do you summarize the worst thing that ever happened to you in a way that makes strangers believe you?

"My name is Olivia Parker."

My voice came out steadier than I expected. Four months of AA meetings had taught me how to speak truth even when it hurt. Especially when it hurt.

"Four months ago, I was raped by Tyler Carrington."

The words felt foreign in my mouth. I'd said them before. To detectives, to doctors, to prosecutors. But this was different. This was for the record. For anyone who would listen.

"His mother is Margaret Carrington, CEO of Carrington Media. She has billions of dollars and an army of lawyers, and they've decided my rape doesn't matter enough to prosecute."

My voice cracked. I cleared my throat. I forced myself to keep going.

"Tyler drugged me. He tied me down with silk scarves that didn't leave marks. He raped me while I couldn't move, couldn't scream, couldn't fight back. And the whole time he played Bach. Classical music. Like what he was doing to me was... refined."

I could still hear it. The violins. The mathematical precision of the notes while everything inside me screamed.

"When I went to the police, when I gave them my rape kit, when I did everything right, it didn't matter. Because he has money and I don't. Because he's powerful and I'm not. Because the system protects men like him and throws away women like me."

Grace kicked against my ribs again. Harder this time. I pressed my hand to my stomach.

"I'm pregnant with his child. I'm four months sober. I'm living with my mother in the house I grew up in, trying to figure out how to be a mother when I can barely take care of myself."

The bathroom was so quiet I could hear water dripping from the faucet. Drip. Drip. Drip. Like a countdown.

"But I need you to know what happened. I need there to be a record. Because someday my daughter is going to ask who her father is. And I need her to know the truth. Not a fairy tale. Not a comfortable lie. The truth."

I stopped. Took a breath.

"Margaret Carrington came to my house three days ago. She offered me two hundred thousand dollars to sign away my voice. To take this baby and disappear. To never tell anyone what her son did to me."

My hands were shaking so hard the phone wobbled. I gripped my knees tighter.

"I said no. I tore up her papers and told her to leave. And she laughed at me. She actually laughed. Like I was the funniest thing she'd seen all year. She said I'd never be able to touch her or her son. That she'd make sure I never work again. That I'm nobody."

I looked straight into the camera. Into my own eyes reflected in the cracked screen.

"Maybe she's right. Maybe I am nobody. A former prostitute with a substance abuse problem and a baby on the way. No money. No job. No prospects."

Grace kicked. Like she disagreed.

"But I'm a nobody who's telling the truth. And someday... I don't know when, I don't know how, but someday I'm going to make sure everyone knows what the Carringtons really are."

I stopped the recording. Stared at the frozen image of my face. Young. Scared. Determined.

I watched it back once. Then twice. Each time seeing something different. The fear in my eyes. The shake in my voice that I'd tried to hide. The way my hand kept moving to my stomach like Grace was the only thing keeping me tethered to this world.

But I also saw something else.

Strength. Raw and unpolished, but real.

I saved it to my phone, naming the file "Grace's Truth.mov" for my daughter to see someday when she was old enough to understand, when she asked the questions I knew were coming.

Then I sat on that bathroom floor, the same floor where I used to hide from Dad's rages, pressing my ear against the cold tiles and praying for it to stop, and cried until I had nothing left.

The tiles were cold against my back. The mirror showed a cracked reflection. Somewhere in the house, I heard Linda moving around the kitchen, making dinner, pretending not to hear me falling apart.

Some things never changed.

I lay in bed that night, hands on my stomach, feeling Grace move. Tiny kicks. Tiny fists. This baby fighting to exist despite everything.

Despite being unwanted by half her DNA. Despite having a mother who could barely keep herself alive, let alone raise a child.

And I made a promise. Not to God this time; I'd stopped believing God listened to people like me. To myself. To my daughter.

I will pay them back. I don't know how. I don't know when. But someday, somehow, I will make the Carringtons answer for what they've done.

Margaret had laughed at me, called me nobody, told me I'd never be able to touch her.

Maybe she was right. But Leo had been nobody too. Just a kid from Millfield with bad choices and worse luck. The men her husband mocked at the Peninsula had been nobody. All the women like me... the desperate, the broken, the ones the system threw away... we were all nobody.

But someday, I would make sure the world knew our names. I would make sure they knew what Margaret and Tyler Carrington really were. Even if it took the rest of my life. Even if it cost me everything I had.

I would find a way. Grace kicked again. Hard. Insistent.

I'm here. I'm fighting. Don't give up.

Pregnant with my rapist's baby. No money. No job. No prospects. But still breathing and still fighting.

And maybe... maybe... that was enough to start with.

Outside, I heard rain start to fall. The kind of steady, soaking rain that Millfield got in late winter, the kind that made everything feel clean for a little while.

I closed my eyes and listened to the rain, feeling my daughter move.

Chapter Three

Three Pounds, Two Ounces

T HE WATER HIT LINDA'S carpet at 2:47 PM on a Tuesday.

I stared down at the wet stain spreading across my sweatpants. Warm. Unstoppable. Wrong. Four weeks too early.

"Mom!"

The word came out like I was six again. High. Panicked. The same voice I'd used when Dad came home drunk and threw plates against the walls.

Linda appeared in the doorway. Her face went white.

"Oh God. Okay. Okay, we're okay." She grabbed my arm. Steady. Strong. "Let's get you to the hospital."

I couldn't move. Couldn't breathe. I was about to have my rapist's baby four weeks before I was ready. If I was ever ready.

"Olivia. Look at me." Linda's hands were on my face. "You can do this."

I wanted to believe her.

Labor hurt like my body was trying to push out something it knew didn't belong. Contractions ripped through me. Sharp. Insistent. Punishment for every bad choice I'd ever made.

The delivery room was too bright. Too cold. Too real. I gripped Linda's hand so tightly I felt her bones shift.

"You're doing great," the nurse said. Lying. Nothing about this was great.

"One more push."

I pushed. Grace was born at 6:47 PM.

Three pounds, two ounces.

The nurse stated it like a fact. Not like a catastrophe. They put Grace on my chest for thirty seconds. That's all I got. Thirty seconds to feel the weight of her. To see her tiny face. To memorize the realness.

She was so small. Smaller than the dolls I'd played with as a child. Fragile. Translucent skin. Eyes closed.

"Hi baby," I whispered. "I'm your—"

And then the alarms started. Loud. Sharp. Piercing.

"She's not breathing."

The nurse's voice was calm. Professional. The kind of calm that means everything is falling apart. They took her.

Hands I didn't know. Scrubs I couldn't identify. My daughter disappearing into a blur of movement and equipment and panic I wasn't allowed to show.

"Wait—" I tried to sit up. Hands pushed me back down. "I didn't... I need to—"

"Let them work." Linda's voice was close to my ear. "They know what they're doing."

Through the chaos, I saw Grace on the table. Tiny body. Unmoving.

Someone pumped her chest with two fingers. Someone else held a mask over her face.

I was screaming, but no sound came out.

Then a cry. Thin. Weak. But alive.

"We've got her." The nurse looked at me. "She's breathing."

They wheeled Grace out before I could touch her again. I lay there in the too-bright room with blood on my legs, milk coming into my breasts, and empty arms that already ached.

Linda was crying. I couldn't. The fear was too overwhelming for tears.

Grace stopped breathing again at 2 AM. The alarms jolted me awake. I ran to the NICU in hospital socks that slipped on the linoleum. Through the glass, I watched them save her.

Again.

Thirty-six hours old, and she'd forgotten how to breathe twice. The NICU nurse, Samantha, her name tag said, saw me standing there. Frozen. Useless.

"She's stable," Samantha said gently. "This happens with preemies."

This happens. As if my daughter dying were routine.

It happened again on day three. The third time in seventy-two hours.

I stood outside the NICU at 4 AM, watching strangers bring my daughter back from wherever babies go when their lungs forget their job.

The NICU smelled like hand sanitizer and desperation. Sharp alcohol cutting through fear. Every parent there had the same hollow eyes. The same silent bargaining with a God who might not be listening.

I couldn't hold Grace. She was in a plastic box with tubes everywhere. In her nose. In her arm. Monitoring things I didn't understand.

A machine breathing for her because her lungs were too small to do it alone. I pressed my hands against the warm plastic. As close as I could get.

"I'm sorry," I whispered. "I'm so sorry."

For drinking before I knew she existed. For being Bob Parker's daughter. For choosing pride over $200,000 that could have paid for everything.

Four months ago, I'd torn up Margaret Carrington's check in front of her face. Now my daughter was dying in a box, and I had $300 in my checking account.

The math was brutal. Pride costs more than I'd calculated.

Dr. Patel came on day fourteen. I knew from her face it was bad.

"Grace has a ventricular septal defect."

The words meant nothing to me. Just syllables.

She showed me a diagram. Pointed to a heart with a hole in it. Blood going the wrong direction. Chambers that couldn't do their job.

"She needs surgery. Soon."

"How soon?"

"Within two weeks. Maybe sooner." Dr. Patel looked at me with kind eyes that I wanted to hate. "The hole isn't closing on its own. We need to repair it surgically or—"

She didn't finish. She didn't have to.

"How much?" My voice sounded far away.

Dr. Patel hesitated. Doctors don't like talking about money. They like pretending healthcare is about healing, not bank accounts.

"The surgery and recovery will cost approximately $180,000."

The number hit like a fist.

"I have three hundred dollars."

Silence.

Dr. Patel's professional mask cracked. Sympathy flooded in.

"I lost my insurance when I got fired." The words tasted like ash. "McKinsey. I had great insurance, but I lost my job and don't have insurance anymore."

"I see." Dr. Patel closed the folder. "Let me talk to our financial counselor. There are programs. Payment plans. We'll figure something out."

But her eyes told the truth. Some things money fixes. And I didn't have any.

I walked back to the NICU on legs that felt unsteady. Through the window, Grace slept in her plastic box. Her tiny chest rose and fell with mechanical precision.

A machine breathing for my daughter while her broken heart tried to remember how to pump blood.

$180,000.

I'd made $150,000 a year at McKinsey, plus a $25,000 signing bonus.

I could have afforded this surgery without blinking. But not anymore.

Linda found me at 3 AM standing outside the NICU. I hadn't moved in two hours.

"Come sit down." She tried to pull me toward the family room.

I couldn't move. Couldn't look away from Grace.

"I should have taken the money," I whispered.

"Don't."

"Two hundred thousand dollars. She offered me two hundred thousand dollars to shut up. I tore it up. I sent it back." My voice cracked. "I chose truth, and now Grace is going to die because I'm too proud to beg."

"She's not going to die."

"How do you know?" I finally looked at Linda. "How do you know that? You can't promise that. Nobody can."

Linda's eyes filled with tears. "You're right. I can't promise. But I know you'll fight for her. Just like you've fought for everything else."

"Fighting doesn't pay for surgery."

"No. But love does."

I didn't understand what she meant. Not yet.

At 3 AM, I stood at the NICU window watching Grace sleep.

The hospital was quiet. Just machines humming. Monitors beeping. Fluorescent lights buzzing like dying insects.

My reflection stared back from the glass. Hollow eyes. Unwashed hair. The ghost of who I used to be.

"I'm sorry," I whispered. The words fogged the glass.

"Your grandmother offered me two hundred thousand dollars. I tore it up." My voice cracked. "I chose truth over your life."

"That's not true."

I spun around. A nurse stood behind me. Older. African American. A kind face with lines that suggested she'd seen everything and chosen kindness anyway.

Her name tag said Samantha. She was the one who had helped save my daughter earlier when Grace couldn't breathe.

"3 AM is when the truth comes out," she said softly. "I've heard worse confessions in this hallway."

We stood in silence, both watching Grace breathe.

"She's a fighter," Samantha said.

"She shouldn't have to be," I replied. "She's three weeks old. She should be safe, not fighting for every breath."

Samantha looked at me. Really looked. "You're sober, aren't you?"

The question hit like a punch. "How did you—"

"Fifteen years." She smiled. Sad. Knowing. "I recognize the guilt. The way you keep waiting for punishment you think you deserve."

My throat closed. "I drank while pregnant. Before I knew. But I did this to her."

"You stopped." Samantha's voice was firm. "That's what matters. You found out and you stopped."

"It was too late."

"Look at her." Samantha pointed at Grace. "Breathing. Fighting. Alive. That's not too late."

I wanted to believe her.

"There's an AA meeting Thursdays in the hospital chapel. 7 AM. You should come."

"I can't leave her—"

"She'll be here. And you'll be stronger for her if you're taking care of yourself." Samantha squeezed my shoulder. "Sobriety isn't just not drinking. It's showing up. Being present."

Then she was gone, leaving me alone with Grace and the machines and a truth I didn't want to accept:

I'd chosen pride, and my daughter might die for it.

Week three, I couldn't sleep. Surgery was scheduled in eight days. Maybe seven. Maybe less if Grace got worse.

I had $300. The hospital needed $180,000. The numbers haunted me. Every time I closed my eyes. Every time I looked at Grace.

At 2 AM, I sat on the bathroom floor scrolling through my phone. I found the confession video I'd recorded months ago: "Grace's ."

I'd filmed it right after the prosecutor dropped the case, right after I realized Tyler would never face consequences.

It was supposed to be for someday, for when Grace was older. Proof that her mother tried. But someday might never come.

If Grace died because I couldn't afford surgery, that video wouldn't matter. My hands shook as I opened the camera app.

The bathroom mirror was unforgiving. The lights revealed every flaw: red eyes from crying, unwashed hair pulled back, no makeup, no filter.

Just desperation. I pressed record.

"My name is Olivia Parker." My voice trembled. I didn't try to hide it. "Three weeks ago, I gave birth to my daughter, Grace."

Deep breath.

"She was born four weeks early, three pounds. She has a ventricular septal defect, a hole in her heart. She needs surgery within the next week. Or she'll die."

I held up the medical paperwork. The numbers looked fake. Too big to be real.

"The surgery costs $180,000. I have $300."

The words hung in the air.

"Eight months ago, I was raped by Tyler Carrington. His mother is Margaret Carrington, CEO of Carrington Media. I reported it to the police, but the prosecutor dropped the charges. Margaret offered me $200,000 to sign an NDA and never speak about what her son did."

My hands were shaking so badly that the camera wobbled.

"I said no because I wanted my daughter to grow up knowing her mother chose truth, that she didn't sell out for money."

I looked directly at the camera.

"But my daughter is dying. And I'm realizing something: integrity doesn't pay for heart surgery. Pride doesn't save lives."

I showed Grace's tiny hand in mine through the NICU glove. So small. So fragile.

"This is Grace. She has a hole in her heart. She needs surgery I can't afford. Not because she did anything wrong, but just because her mother was too proud to stay silent."

I wiped my eyes. Tears kept falling.

"I'm not asking for justice anymore. I tried that. The system doesn't work for people like me. I'm just asking for help. For her."

Samantha had helped me set up a GoFundMe link earlier that day. I showed it to the camera.

"If you can donate anything... a dollar, five dollars... it matters. And if you can't donate, please share this. My daughter shouldn't die because I chose principle over pragmatism."

I stopped recording and stared at the screen. This was it. My last option. My only option. Begging strangers on the internet to save my daughter's life.

I posted it to YouTube at 3:47 AM. Then I sat in the dark bathroom and cried until Linda found me at dawn.

Nothing happened.

Six hours later: 37 views. $15 donated.

I refreshed the page obsessively, watching the numbers, willing them to move. Each view felt like a miracle. Each dollar a lifeline I was desperately grasping.

By noon: 52 views. $15.

The number hadn't changed.

"It's not working," I told Samantha in the NICU family room.

"Give it time."

"Grace doesn't have time." My voice was rising, panic creeping in. "Surgery is in seven days. We need $180,000."

"Then we pray," Samantha said simply.

But I'd never been good at prayer.

By 6 PM: 200 views. $43.

Forty-three dollars.

I sat staring at the screen, fighting the urge to scream. This wasn't working. Nobody cared. Nobody was going to save us.

I'd humiliated myself. Begged the internet for nothing. Then, my phone buzzed. A notification. Someone had posted my video on Reddit.

r/TwoXChromosomes.

The title made my stomach turn: "Former McKinsey consultant raped by billionaire's son, prosecutor drops case, now her baby is dying."

It was clickbait. But it was also true. I clicked on the comments. They were tearing me apart.

"This is fake. Total scam."

"She's exploiting her daughter for money."

"The rape allegations were investigated and dropped. She's a liar."

My hands shook. This was a mistake. A terrible mistake. But then I kept scrolling.

"I was raped by a wealthy man too. No one believed me either."

"My sister had a baby with a heart defect. The costs are real. This is real."

"Just donated. Fuck the Carringtons and screw the prosecutors who protect rich rapists."

The donations started moving.

$43 became $156. Then $340. Then $891.

I couldn't look away from the screen. By midnight: 15,000 views. $2,127 raised.

I sat in the dark NICU watching the numbers climb, crying, unable to believe it was real. Strangers were helping me.

People I'd never meet were choosing to believe me.

Day two, I woke to 147 missed calls. Journalists, TV stations, bloggers. Everyone wanting the story.

"Is this real?"

"Can you verify the rape allegation?"

"Will you come on camera?"

I said no to all of them. I wasn't ready to be a story. I didn't want to be inspiration porn for people who had never been where I was.

I just wanted Grace to live. But they wrote about it anyway.

Twitter exploded. Someone with 50,000 followers retweeted the video. Then someone with 200,000.

"McKinsey Consultant Claims Rape by Media Mogul's Son; Baby Needs Life-Saving Surgery."

The headline spread like wildfire. Then Carrington Media responded. Their PR statement dropped at 2 PM:

"These allegations are unsubstantiated. Ms. Parker's claims were investigated by law enforcement and deemed insufficient for prosecution. We are saddened that she is exploiting her premature infant's medical condition for financial gain and to advance false narratives against the Carrington family."

I read it three times. I felt sick. They were calling me a liar in front of millions of people. They were saying I was using my dying daughter as a prop.

I showed the statement to Samantha, my hands shaking so badly I almost dropped my phone.

"They're going to destroy me," I whispered. "Everyone's going to believe them."

Samantha read it, then looked at me.

"You're telling the truth, right?"

"Yes."

"Then the truth will win."

The statement backfired. People don't like billionaires calling desperate mothers liars. The comments section turned into a war zone:

"Carrington Media just proved she's telling the truth. They're scared."

"Rich people always silence victims with money and lawyers. Not this time."

"The fact that they responded at all means they're worried. Donating now."

The donations doubled and then tripled.

By the end of day two: 150,000 views, $18,473 raised. I couldn't process the numbers. They didn't feel real. But Grace's surgery was in five days.

We still needed $161,527.

Day three, a news van showed up in the hospital parking lot.

I refused the interview. I hid in the NICU. But they filmed the exterior anyway and ran a segment on the evening news.

"Local woman claims billionaire's son raped her. Now her premature baby needs expensive heart surgery she can't afford."

They showed my LinkedIn photo. Professional. Smiling. The McKinsey consultant who had everything. Then my mugshot from the DUI. Hollow eyes. Broken.

Then Tyler Carrington appeared at a charity gala. Tuxedo. Wine glass. Smiling like he'd never hurt anyone. The visual contrast did what I couldn't. It made people believe.

By day four: 500,000 views. $75,328 raised.

Halfway there. I allowed myself to hope for the first time. Maybe we'd make it. Maybe strangers really were going to save my daughter's life.

Then the cease-and-desist letter arrived.

A letter from Carrington Media's legal team at 9 PM on day four. Legal language I barely understood. Threats about defamation. Demands to remove the video immediately. Warning of criminal prosecution if I didn't comply.

I sat in the NICU family room reading it over and over. They were going to sue me. Take what little I had left. Destroy me completely.

Samantha found me crying at midnight.

"What happened?"

I showed her the letter. My hands wouldn't stop shaking.

"They want me to take the video down. They're threatening to sue me for defamation."

"Are you lying?" Samantha asked.

"No."

"Then don't take it down."

"I don't have a lawyer. I don't have money for a lawyer. They'll destroy me."

"They're already trying to destroy you." Samantha's voice was steady. Certain. "But you're telling the truth. They can't stop the truth."

"They can if they have better lawyers."

"Maybe." Samantha sat down next to me. "But right now, you have something they don't."

"What?"

"People who believe you."

I didn't take the video down.

By day five: 750,000 views. $112,847 raised.

Day six: 1,000,000 views. $158,293 raised.

So close. So impossibly close. Grace's surgery was scheduled for tomorrow morning. We needed $21,707 more. I stayed up all night watching the numbers.

Refresh. Refresh. Refresh.

$158,500.

$159,012.

$159,847.

Each donation felt like a prayer answered. Each dollar a stranger saying: You matter. She matters.

At 6:47 AM on day seven, exactly three weeks after Grace was born, we hit the goal.

$180,000.

I stared at the screen, unable to move. Unable to breathe. The number didn't look real.

8,347 donors. People I'd never meet. Would never be able to thank properly. They'd read my story and decided it mattered.

My daughter mattered. Linda found me sobbing in the NICU bathroom.

"What's wrong?"

I couldn't speak. I just showed her my phone. She read the number and started crying too.

"Oh baby. Oh my sweet baby." We held each other in the hospital bathroom and cried.

Not from sadness. From the impossible weight of strangers' kindness.

The video had been viewed 1.2 million times. Comments flooded in by the hundreds:

"My daughter had the same surgery ten years ago. She's healthy now. You'll get through this."

"I believe you about the rape. I believe all of you. Stay strong."

"Donated $500. Fuck the Carringtons and everyone who protects rapists."

"You're so brave. Your daughter is lucky to have you."

I wasn't brave. I was desperate. But maybe that's what bravery looks like from the outside.

Desperation choosing to fight instead of surrender. I sat in the NICU staring at the staggering number.

$180,000.

Strangers had saved my daughter's life. I'd humiliated myself. Begged the internet. Shared my worst moments. And somehow, impossibly, people had chosen to help. Not because they knew me, but because they believed me.

Grace's surgery was scheduled for 8 AM. Twelve hours from now. And for the first time in three weeks, I let myself believe she might survive.

At 3 AM, three hours before surgery, a woman approached me in the NICU waiting room.

Young. Maybe twenty-three. Scared eyes. Twisting her hands.

"Olivia Parker?"

I nodded. Barely.

"I'm sorry to bother you. I just... I wanted to say thank you."

"You donated?" My voice was hoarse from crying.

"Five dollars. That's all I could afford." She looked ashamed. "But I meant thank you for something else."

She sat down. Uninvited but somehow welcome.

"My boyfriend raped me six months ago. I didn't report it. He's a lawyer. I'm a waitress. I thought no one would believe me."

Tears streamed down her face.

"But you proved something. You proved you can speak up even when they're powerful. Even when the system fails. Even when it costs everything."

She wiped her eyes.

"You proved truth matters. Even when it doesn't win."

I didn't feel like I'd proved anything. I'd begged strangers for money. Lost my dignity. Shared my daughter's medical crisis with the world. But looking at her face, I saw something I hadn't expected:

Hope. She stood to leave.

"Your daughter is going to make it," she said. "I know she will. Because mothers like you don't give up."

Then, she was gone. And I sat alone in the waiting room at 3 AM, realizing something:

Maybe my failure to get justice could still mean something. Maybe sharing the truth mattered even when it didn't change the outcome.

Grace's surgery started in five hours. And for the first time since she was born, I felt something besides fear:

Gratitude. For a daughter who fought every day to breathe. For $180,000 raised dollar by dollar by strangers who decided my daughter's life mattered.

I pressed my hands against the NICU glass and watched Grace sleep.

"We're going to make it," I whispered. "Somehow, we're going to make it."

And for the first time, I believed it.

The surgery took four hours. Four hours of sitting in a waiting room that smelled like stale coffee and fear. Four hours of watching the clock, imagining every worst-case scenario, and making bargains with a God I wasn't sure existed.

Linda sat beside me. We didn't talk. We just held hands and breathed.

Please. Please. It was the only prayer I knew.

Dr. Patel appeared in the doorway at 12:43 PM.

Her face was gray. My stomach dropped through the floor.

"She's alive."

The words came fast and urgent, as if she knew what I was thinking. But her face told a different story.

"What happened?" My voice didn't sound like mine.

Linda's hand gripped mine so tightly that our bones ground together. Dr. Patel sat down. Doctors don't sit down for good news.

"The surgery was successful. We repaired the defect. Grace is stable."

"But?"

"She flatlined during the procedure."

The room tilted.

"What?"

"Her heart stopped for eight seconds. We got her back."

Eight seconds. Grace had been dead for eight seconds. My daughter had died on that table.

"Eight seconds?" I couldn't breathe. Couldn't think. "She was dead?"

"Technically, yes. But we got her back immediately. It's not uncommon in surgeries like this—"

"She died." The words came out flat. Final.

Linda was crying beside me. I couldn't.

The shock was too big for tears.

"She's stable now," Dr. Patel said gently. "Breathing on her own. Heart functioning normally. The surgery was successful."

"But she died."

"For eight seconds. And now she's alive." Dr. Patel leaned forward. "Olivia, your daughter is going to be okay."

I nodded, but the words wouldn't sink in. Grace had died. For eight seconds, my daughter's heart had stopped beating. And I hadn't been there.

Grace came home on a Tuesday in December.

Six months old. Healthy. Thriving. The scar on her chest had faded to a thin white line. Still visible. Still there. A reminder that she had fought and won.

Linda's guest room was full of donated equipment: a bassinet missing one wheel, clothes from the church thrift store, and toys that had belonged to other children. But it was ours.

I sat in the old rocking chair, the same one Linda had used when I was a baby to hold my daughter while she slept.

The house was quiet, just the sound of Grace breathing: steady, strong.

Outside, December rain fell. Cold and cleansing, the kind of winter rain that made everything feel new.

I looked down at Grace, at her chest rising and falling, fixed and strong, and at her tiny fingers wrapped around mine. The daughter strangers had saved.

"I promise," I whispered in the darkness.

Grace stirred but didn't wake.

"I promise I'll teach you to fight, that truth matters, and that you're worth more than any amount of silence money."

My voice cracked.

"I couldn't save Leo. I tried. I failed. He died believing I'd save him, and I couldn't."

Tears slipped down my face.

"But I saved you."

The rain fell harder. Steady. Relentless.

I thought about the video, about the strangers who had believed me, about the mothers messaging me for help. Something was starting; I could feel it.

I didn't know what yet. But holding Grace in the darkness, listening to the rain, I made another promise:

If I had learned how to make people care enough to save my daughter, maybe I could help others too. Not tonight. Not tomorrow. But someday. When Grace was stronger. When I was stronger.

I rocked my daughter in Linda's old chair, listened to her breathe, and felt her warmth.

"We're going to be okay," I whispered. "I don't know how. I don't know what comes next. But we're going to be okay."

Grace's hand tightened around my finger in her sleep. And I sat in the darkness holding the most precious thing I had ever fought for.

The rain washed everything clean. Tomorrow would come. But tonight, I just held my daughter. And that was everything.

Chapter Four

The Public Eye

GRACE WAS SIX MONTHS old, and three thousand strangers were asking if she was still alive.

I sat in Linda's dark kitchen at 2 AM with my daughter asleep on my chest, scrolling through messages from people I'd never meet. Eight thousand three hundred forty-seven of them had opened their wallets when I had nothing left. They had believed me when Margaret Carrington called me a liar. They had saved Grace's life with their credit cards and their faith that maybe truth mattered.

They deserved to know if it worked.

I propped my phone against Linda's sugar bowl. The ceramic was cold. The kitchen smelled like old coffee and lavender dish soap. Normal smells from a life that used to feel safe.

Hit record.

"Hi everyone." My voice cracked immediately. I didn't try to hide it. "I don't know how to thank you for saving her."

Grace stirred against me, her tiny fist grabbing my shirt.

I tilted the camera to show them the scar, that thin white line down her chest where surgeons had cut her open and sewn her heart back together with eight thousand people's money.

"She's alive because of you."

Tears blurred everything, and I let them fall.

"I can't thank eight thousand people individually, but I'm trying. We're here because of you."

I posted it at 3:47 AM, the same time as the original desperate video. I didn't realize I was creating a ritual until later.

I woke four hours later to my phone vibrating off the nightstand. Fifty thousand views. By the time Grace finished nursing: one hundred thousand. Comments were scrolling so fast I couldn't read them all.

We love her.

Thank you for updating us.

Please don't leave us. Keep posting.

You're helping me survive my son's NICU stay right now.

They didn't just want to know she lived. They wanted more. They wanted to keep being part of Grace's story. They wanted me to keep showing them my daughter.

Over the next two weeks, I kept posting because I didn't know what else to do. Grace's first real smile. Her morning routines. Her frustrated attempts to roll over. Each video got more views and more comments begging me not to stop.

Then, one Tuesday in February, Grace rolled over for the first time while I was filming. I watched it happen through my phone screen, not with my actual eyes, not with the presence a mother should have.

I realized it three seconds too late. I stopped recording, picked Grace up, and held her close while she squirmed, proud of what she'd done.

"I'm sorry," I whispered into her hair.

I posted the video that night. Two hundred thousand views. *You're such a good mom for capturing the moment.*

If they only knew.

I didn't film for three days after that. I couldn't make myself do it. The subscriber count dropped, views tanked, and my inbox filled with worried messages.

Linda found me Saturday morning, staring at analytics showing the decline.

"If I stop posting, they forget us," I said. "And if they forget us, we're back in the shelter."

I started filming again that night. I had to. There wasn't another choice.

The email from YouTube arrived on Valentine's Day: "Monetization Eligibility."

I stared at it for three days. They wanted to pay me for views, for ads playing before videos of Grace recovering from heart surgery. It felt like selling something I couldn't get back.

Linda found me Thursday night at the kitchen table, Grace asleep upstairs, and my laptop open to the email I'd been avoiding.

"What's stopping you?"

"Margaret said I was exploiting Grace. If I click this button, she's right."

Linda was quiet for a long moment. The kitchen was dark except for my laptop screen. Outside, the February wind rattled the windows.

"Margaret offered you two hundred thousand to hide," Linda finally said. "You tore up the check because silence was wrong. Now YouTube wants to pay you to keep talking, to keep being visible. How is that the same?"

"Because I'm making money from Grace—"

"From surviving, from documenting your daughter's recovery, from being honest." Linda leaned forward. "Money doesn't make something wrong, baby. How you get it does."

My finger hovered over the trackpad.

"What if Grace grows up and hates me for this?"

"Maybe she will," Linda said quietly. "But maybe she'll understand you did the best you could. That you refused to let Margaret win."

I clicked.

Your application has been submitted. You'll hear back within 30 days.

I closed the laptop. It felt like I'd crossed a line I'd been trying not to cross.

Thirty days later: *Payment received: $127.43*

One hundred twenty-seven dollars. For views. For ads. For letting strangers watch my daughter grow up.

I sat on those cold tiles, the same floor I'd learned to hide on as a child when Dad's rages got too loud, and cried. Not from shame. From relief so overwhelming I couldn't breathe.

This was real money. Money I hadn't earned by selling my body at truck stops. Money that appeared just for being honest.

Next payment: $340. Month after: $890.

Each one felt like proof we might actually survive.

The first time I left the house after the payments started, I went to Target. Linda practically pushed me out the door. The store was overwhelming, too bright, too many people, but I found myself in the baby section holding a white onesie. $8.99.

When was the last time I'd bought something new? Before McKinsey fired me. Before the shelter. Before I learned that new things were for people who mattered.

The cashier smiled. "How old?"

"Six months."

"First baby?"

"Yeah."

She didn't see a homeless person. Didn't see a rape victim. Just saw a tired mom buying her baby something nice.

For the first time in a year, I felt normal.

I walked to Linda's car, crying so hard I could barely see. $127 from YouTube had bought me that feeling.

Grace wore the onesie in the next video. Comments asked where I got it. I linked it. Made $4 in affiliate commissions. I started understanding what money meant. Not freedom exactly. Possibility. The feeling I could buy Grace something new tomorrow without calculating whether we'd eat.

Company emails started arriving. Free products to review. Then bigger offers: *We'd love to sponsor a video. $500 for eight minutes.*

Five hundred dollars. I'd made $150,000 a year at McKinsey. Now $500 felt impossible.

That night I made a list in my old notebook: 100,000 subscribers by summer. $8,000/month income. Save for an apartment deposit. Build something Margaret can't silence.

I stared at that last line. That one was war.

The ring light arrived in April. Thirty dollars on Amazon. I set it up in Linda's guest room and turned it on. Harsh brightness flooded the space. Grace was on the floor. She squinted and turned her face away from the light.

I should have turned it off. Should have returned it. Instead, I angled it slightly and kept filming.

Grace fussed the entire eight minutes, making uncomfortable noises. She reached toward me as if she wanted to be picked up, away from the light didn't hurt her eyes.

I kept filming. I got what I needed. I turned it off.

Grace stopped fussing immediately. She looked at me as if she was trying to understand something.

I looked away. I posted the video that night, hating myself. But the analytics were clear: 50,000 more views than usual. *Your lighting is amazing! Videos keep getting better!*

I started filming with the ring light regularly. Grace would fuss. I'd film faster. The videos performed better. More views meant more money, which meant moving out sooner.

So I kept doing it.

Linda found me at 3 AM one night. The ring light was blazing. Grace was crying from the brightness. I was filming anyway because I'd missed Tuesday's upload, and the algorithm punished inconsistency.

"Olivia. It's 3 AM. Grace is crying."

"I know. Almost done—"

Linda crossed the room and switched off the light. Darkness fell. Grace stopped crying immediately.

"You need to sleep."

"I need to post. If I don't—"

"You're killing yourself for YouTube videos." Linda's voice cracked. "You haven't left this house in two weeks. You're filming at 3 AM with a light that hurts her eyes."

"I'm trying to survive—"

"At what cost? At the cost of being present with Grace?"

"At the cost of not living in shelters! Not going back to truck stops! Not selling myself to stay alive!"

Silence stretched between us.

"I know you're scared," Linda said softly. "But if this is what survival looks like—"

"There is no different way. This is all I have."

She took Grace from my arms and told me to sleep for two hours.

I collapsed onto the bed. When I woke, I checked the analytics immediately. The video I'd missed on Tuesday had views down 30%. The algorithm had already started deprioritizing my channel.

I turned the ring light back on that night.

Grace started sitting up in late April. Wobbly, she fell over every few seconds. I filmed her trying, failing, catching herself, and trying again. My heart ached watching her determination. She was seven months old and already better at fighting than I'd ever be.

I posted it Saturday night: *Grace's First Time Sitting (Mostly Falling)*

I woke Sunday to my phone exploding. Three hundred thousand views and climbing. By Monday: five hundred thousand. By Tuesday: one million.

The kind of viral moment creators dream about.

Wednesday morning, Linda handed me her iPad at breakfast. Her face was tight with worry.

"You need to see this."

The Dark Side of GoFundMe: When Trauma Becomes Content

My body started shaking before I finished the first paragraph.

A young mother has turned her premature infant's medical crisis into a lucrative content empire, documenting every moment of her child's recovery for clicks and advertising revenue.

While she claims to be "helping other mothers," critics question whether constant filming serves the child's best interests or simply the parent's bottom line.

The article continued. Timeline of my videos. View counts. Estimated earnings. Terrifyingly close to accurate. Quote from a "media ethics expert": *"When a child's trauma becomes content for profit, we must seriously question the parent's motives."*

My toast rose in my throat. "It's not true," I whispered.

"I know, baby."

I scrolled to the bottom. Googled the publication. Subsidiary of Carrington Media.

"She found me."

The articles multiplied quickly.

Thursday: three more publications, all Carrington-connected. Friday: seven. All calling me an exploiter without naming me directly. My comment sections started filling with attacks.

Exploiter.

Bad mother.

Using that poor baby.

But that was just the warm-up.

Monday morning, Linda showed me a YouTube video:

"The TRUTH About Grace's Mom: Investigation"

A channel called TruthSeeker, with half a million subscribers, had made a twenty-minute deep dive. Professional production. Serious music. Charts and graphs showing my estimated earnings. Timeline of when I started monetizing.

"She raised $180,000 for a surgery that cost $180,000. But she's still making money off Grace six months later. Where's that money going?"

The video had 400,000 views in two days.

Tuesday, Drama Alert picked it up. Two million subscribers. "YouTuber Accused of Exploiting Sick Baby for Profit."

Wednesday, a third channel: "I Investigated Grace's Mom and What I Found is DISTURBING."

Each one bigger than the last. Each one making everything look calculated. Predatory. Evil. Like I'd planned Grace's heart defect as a content opportunity.

My comment sections turned into war zones:

How do you sleep at night?

Someone needs to call CPS on this woman.

I'm unsubscribing. This is sick.

Subscriber count Tuesday: 103,000. Wednesday: 98,000. Thursday: 92,000. Friday: 85,000.

Hemorrhaging thousands every day. Views tanked. Videos that used to get 200,000 now struggled to reach 50,000.

Sponsorship companies started emailing. *We need to pause our partnership given the recent concerns.* A professional way of saying: we don't want to be associated with you.

I watched my income collapse in real time. March: $4,200. April projection based on current numbers: maybe $2,000. Not enough for an apartment deposit. Not enough for anything except barely surviving in Linda's guest room.

Thursday night, I had my first panic attack.

Grace was asleep. I was reading comments. I couldn't stop reading them even though each one felt like a knife.

Your daughter will hate you someday.

You're a monster.

Child Protective Services needs to take that baby away.

My chest tightened. I couldn't breathe. The room started spinning. My heart pounded so hard I thought it would explode out of my chest.

I stumbled to the bathroom. Pressed my face against the cold tile. Gasped for air that wouldn't come.

This was it. Margaret was winning. She'd destroyed me without even trying. She simply weaponized the internet against me and watched me burn.

And maybe she was right. Maybe I was a monster.

Linda found me on the floor twenty minutes later. I still couldn't breathe properly.

"Baby, breathe. With me. In. Out."

It took thirty minutes before I could stand.

"They're right," I whispered. "I am using her."

"You're not—"

"I am! I film her when she's uncomfortable. I choose money over her comfort. How is that not exploitation?"

Linda held me. She didn't have an answer because there wasn't a good one.

The panic attacks became daily.

Friday morning, I was reading comments. My chest tightened. I couldn't breathe.

Saturday afternoon, the subscriber count dropped below 80,000. I had a panic attack in the kitchen while Grace played on the floor, oblivious to her mother falling apart.

Sunday, another investigatory video dropped. This one found old photos of me from McKinsey. Professional headshots. It made it look like I'd had this perfect life and thrown it away for YouTube money.

"She went from a six-figure salary to monetizing her daughter's medical trauma. What does that tell you?"

The panic attack lasted an hour. Linda found me shaking so hard my teeth chattered.

"You need to stop reading comments."

"I can't. I need to know what they're saying—"

"You need to breathe. That's all."

But I had to keep checking. Every morning, the first thing I did was check the subscriber count, check views, read comments, and watch my life disintegrate.

Grace started crying more, picking up on my anxiety. She was clingy, fussy, and not sleeping, which made me feel worse. I was doing this to her. My panic was hurting her just like my filming had.

Everything I did hurt her.

Monday: 78,000 subscribers.

Tuesday: Views on the new video barely broke 40,000.

Wednesday: Income projection for April: $1,800.

Not enough. Back to nothing after all of this.

That night, after Linda went to bed and after Grace finally fell asleep following two hours of fussiness, I sat in the dark kitchen with my phone.

Margaret is winning.

I knew it. I'd always known it, hadn't I?

You can't beat people like the Carringtons. They have too much power, too much money, and too many ways to destroy you without even getting their hands dirty.

I stood up, grabbed my keys from the counter, and my jacket from the hook by the door.

There was a 7-Eleven three blocks away, open twenty-four hours. I'd driven past it every day for months without thinking about it.

Now, I couldn't think about anything else.

My feet moved before I decided to move them. Out the door, down Linda's driveway. The street was empty and dark, the kind of dark that makes bad decisions feel invisible.

The walk took five minutes. It felt like five seconds.

The fluorescent lights inside made me squint. Too bright. Too clean. A kid behind the counter couldn't have been more than twenty and barely looked up from his phone.

I walked to the back, to the alcohol section. Rows and rows of bottles: beer, wine, hard liquor.

There. Smirnoff. Just like Dad used to drink.

I picked up the bottle. Plastic. Cheap. The weight was familiar in my hand even after four hundred sixty-three days.

I carried it to the counter and set it down.

The kid scanned it. "ID?"

I fumbled for my wallet. He barely glanced at it, took my card, and swiped it.

"Receipt?"

"No."

He bagged it in brown paper, as if that made it less obvious what it was.

I walked out, the bottle heavy in my hand. Heavier than it should have been.

The walk back felt longer. Each step was a choice. I could turn around, go back, return it, say I'd made a mistake.

But I didn't.

Linda's house was dark when I got there. I let myself in quietly and set the bag on the counter.

I found a glass in the cabinet. One of Linda's everyday glasses. Clear. Simple. Used to hold orange juice and milk and other normal things.

I unscrewed the cap. The seal broke with a crack. I poured. The vodka caught the streetlight coming through the window. Clear. Clean-looking. Deceptive.

The smell hit me immediately. Sharp. Chemical. Underneath it, something sweet. Something that smelled like relief and forgetting and every bad decision I'd ever made.

I picked up the glass and held it close to my face, letting the fumes burn my nose.

Just one drink. That's all it would take.

I raised the glass to my lips.

A sound from upstairs. Grace. A soft whimper through the baby monitor on the counter. Not crying yet. Just stirring.

My hand stopped, the vodka an inch from my mouth.

Another whimper. Louder.

I set the glass down.

Grace would wake up soon. She'd cry. And I'd go upstairs. Would I go upstairs drunk? Would I stumble through her door smelling like vodka? Would I pick her up and tell myself it was just one drink, just one, like Dad used to say?

I looked at my reflection in the window. Distorted. Dark. Barely recognizable.

Dad chose alcohol over us every single day. Every birthday. Every Christmas. Every time I begged him to stop.

Was I choosing it now?

I thought about Easter Sunday. That bathroom floor. Six years old in my Easter dress. Cleaning up Dad's vomit because Mom was too scared to touch him.

Sitting on that cold tile floor and making a promise.

Dear God, I will never, ever, EVER be like my father.

I'd meant it with everything in me. I'd kept that promise for fifteen years. Until Leo died. Until I became exactly what I'd promised I'd never be.

But I'd fought my way back. Four hundred sixty-three days of fighting. Of choosing to feel everything instead of numbing it.

If I drank this now, what would that say to that six-year-old girl on the bathroom floor? The one who deserved a father who chose her over alcohol?

Grace made another sound. A little cry this time. Waking up.

I looked at the glass. At the vodka waiting. Then I looked at the baby monitor. Real. Immediate. Needing me.

My hands were shaking. The glass trembled.

Grace cried louder. That full cry now.

I walked to the sink and poured it out, watching the vodka swirl down the drain. Clear. Harmless-looking. Gone.

I poured the rest of the bottle after it. Every drop. Until it was empty. I threw the bottle in the trash. The glass clinked loudly in the quiet kitchen.

Grace was screaming now. I ran upstairs.

She was on her back in the bassinet, face red, fists clenched. That thin white scar was visible even in the dim light.

I picked her up. "I'm here," I whispered. "Mama's here."

She kept crying, not calming down right away. Just cried and cried like she knew.

I walked her around the room, swaying and humming. My voice was shaky.

Slowly, she quieted, making that little hiccup sound she always made after crying hard.

I held her tighter, pressing my face against her head. She smelled like baby shampoo and innocence.

"I'm sorry," I whispered.

I carried her to the rocking chair. She was already falling back asleep, her body heavy against my chest. Trusting.

That six-year-old girl on the bathroom floor had made a promise. I'd broken it once, but I was keeping it now.

I'd made my choice, and it wasn't the vodka. It was this. This baby in my arms. This choosing to feel everything instead of numbing it.

Still sober. Still choosing. Still fighting.

That had to count for something.

Chapter Five

First Blood

THE CUSTODY PETITION ARRIVED on a Wednesday in late June. The envelope sat on the kitchen table. White. Official. Like a bomb wrapped in paper.

I stared at it for twenty minutes before finally opening the envelope. My hands were shaking so badly that I tore the paper.

Petition for Custody and Visitation Rights.

Tyler Carrington, plaintiff, requests supervised visitation with minor child Grace Parker.

The words swam. My heart pounded in my ears. He wanted to see her. The man who raped me wanted to see our daughter.

I made it to the bathroom before I threw up.

I called Patricia with trembling fingers.

"Can he do this?"

"Yes." Her voice was tired. Professional. "He's the biological father. He has parental rights under Illinois law."

"He raped me!!"

Grace started crying in the other room. My scream had scared her.

"The criminal case was dropped," Patricia said, calm, as if this were normal. "The settlement resolved your civil claims. But parental rights are separate. He has the right to petition for visitation."

"So he just... gets to do this? After what he did?"

"He's claiming he's completed treatment. He has evidence of sobriety, anger management, therapy. The court will likely consider his request."

"I can't let him near her."

"Olivia." Patricia's voice was gentle now. "You need to prepare yourself. The court looks at the best interests of the child. Legally, that includes access to both parents when possible."

"He's a rapist."

"He's also never been convicted of a crime. That's the reality we're working with."

Grace was still crying. I went to her and picked her up from the playpen. She was so small. So fragile. Her little body tense with fear.

She made sounds. Not words. Just scared baby noises.

I held her and tried to breathe, trying to figure out how to protect her from the monster who made her.

The custody hearing was two weeks later, on a Tuesday morning in July.

I didn't sleep the night before. I just lay in bed staring at the ceiling. My chest was so tight I thought I might suffocate.

Linda came with me and held my hand in the car.

"You don't have to do this alone," she said.

But I did have to do it alone. Because no one else could fight for Grace the way I could. No one else knew what Tyler really was.

The courthouse smelled like pine cleaner. Chemical-sweet. Fake. Just like his apartment.

My stomach turned the moment I walked in. The smell was everywhere. In my nose. In my throat. In my brain. I gripped Linda's hand harder.

You're safe. You're in a courthouse. He can't touch you here.

But my body didn't believe me. We sat at a table with Patricia. Tyler sat across the courtroom with his lawyer.

I forced myself to look at him. He was wearing a navy suit. Expensive. Hair perfectly combed. Not a strand out of place.

A white shirt underneath.

The white shirt.

My throat closed up. He was smoothing it as he sat down, palms flat against the fabric. The ritual. His eyes caught mine for just a second.

Empty eyes. The same eyes that had stared at me while he counted how many times I said please.

His lawyer was a woman. Sharp suit. Sharp voice. She presented evidence like she was selling a product.

"Mr. Carrington has completed six months of intensive treatment at Wellspring Recovery Center. He's maintained complete sobriety, attended anger management courses, and engaged in therapy twice weekly. He's employed at Carrington Media in a stable position. He's done everything the court could ask of him."

She pulled out documents. Certificates. Letters from therapists.

"Mr. Carrington deeply regrets the circumstances that led to Ms. Parker's allegations. But he has worked hard to become a better person, and he has the right to know his daughter."

Allegations. Like I made it up. Like he didn't drug me, tie me down, and rape me while Bach played and I floated above my own body.

My turn came. I sat on the witness stand. The room was too bright. Too hot.

Patricia asked questions. I answered them.

But I could feel Tyler watching me. His cologne drifted across the courtroom. Expensive. Heavy. The same smell from that night.

My hands gripped the chair, my knuckles white.

Don't throw up. Don't throw up. Don't panic.

I told them about the drugged wine, about waking up with hours missing from my life, about the rape kit, the DNA match, the prosecutor who believed me but couldn't file charges because of who he was.

Tyler's lawyer cross-examined me. Brought up my prostitution record, my homelessness, my drinking.

"Ms. Parker has a history of making poor decisions. How can we trust her judgment about co-parenting?"

The room spun. She was making me the dangerous one.

Not Tyler. Not the rapist. Me.

During a break, I had to use the bathroom. My legs were shaking. Each step down that hallway felt wrong. Too exposed.

Then I saw him.

Tyler. Twenty feet away. Standing there like he'd been waiting.

His lawyer was gone. The bailiff was gone. Nobody watching. Nobody between us.

His face changed.

The professional mask, the one he'd worn all morning in court, just slipped off. Like taking off a jacket. Easy. Natural.

He smiled.

Not the practiced courtroom smile he'd shown the judge. Something else. Something that made my stomach drop.

Cold. Sharp. Pleased.

He looked at me the way a cat looks at a mouse. Like he was remembering. Like he was enjoying the memory.

My hand flew to my throat. I didn't mean to do it. Didn't think about it. My fingers just went there. Pressed against the skin.

And I felt it.

His hands. Wrapping around my neck. Squeezing. The pressure building until I couldn't breathe, couldn't scream, couldn't do anything but make those animal sounds while the Bach played and he counted how many times I said please.

The phantom sensation was so real I gasped.

My throat burned like it had that morning. Raw. Damaged. Purple fingerprints ringed around it like a necklace I never wanted.

Tyler smoothed his white shirt. Slow. Deliberate. Palms flat against the fabric. Checking the creases.

The ritual. My legs almost gave out.

He was showing me. Reminding me. Making sure I knew he remembered that night too. Making sure I understood he was thinking about it right now. About the drugged wine. The silk scarves. My body that wouldn't move while my mind screamed.

I stumbled into the bathroom. Shoved the door open so hard it slammed against the wall. Locked myself in a stall. Sat on the toilet lid.

My hand was still pressed against my throat. I could feel my pulse hammering under my fingers. Fast. Terrified.

That look. That smile. He wasn't better. Wasn't reformed. Wasn't the changed man his therapist's letters claimed he was.

He was the same monster. Just better at hiding it. And nobody else had seen. Nobody else knew.

They'd all watched him in that courtroom. The polished businessman in the expensive suit. The reformed addict who went to therapy twice a week, completed anger management, and said all the right things.

They didn't see the predator in the hallway. The one who looked at me like he wanted to do it again. Like terrorizing me was entertainment.

I pressed harder against my throat, trying to ground myself, trying to remember this was now, not then; that I was dressed, not tied down; that the Bach wasn't playing.

But my throat remembered. My body remembered.

The pressure of his fingers. The way I couldn't scream. The hours that went missing while he used me, and I floated above my own body, watching, helpless.

I made it back to the courtroom somehow.

Patricia leaned over. "You okay? You're white as a sheet."

I couldn't tell her. Couldn't explain what I'd seen. What I'd felt. My hand was still at my throat. I made myself drop it, putting it in my lap where she couldn't see it shaking.

The judge called Tyler to the stand. He walked up there calm and confident, answering questions in that formal, measured voice he'd practiced with his lawyers.

"I deeply regret the pain I've caused Ms. Parker. I was struggling with addiction and mental health issues at the time. I've since committed myself to treatment and personal growth."

Lies. All lies.

My fingernails were cutting into my palms. The other hand kept wanting to go back to my throat. To check. To feel.

"I want to be a father to Grace. I want to support her, love her, be present in her life."

I pressed my hand flat against the table, forcing it to stay there.

"I understand Ms. Parker's concerns. But I've changed. I'm not that person anymore."

He looked at the judge. Sincere. Honest. The mask perfect. Then his eyes slid to me, just for a second.

There it was again.

That cold smile. That pleased look. Like this was all a game he was winning. Like remembering what he did to me was fun.

Then it vanished. The mask back in place. Professional. Reformed. Safe.

The judge shuffled papers, looked at Tyler, then looked at me.

"This is a complex case. I'm not prepared to make a final ruling today."

Hope flared in my chest.

"However." He looked at Tyler. "Mr. Carrington, you've presented compelling evidence of rehabilitation. I'll make my final decision in three months. Both parties will submit additional documentation."

The gavel came down. Not final yet. But close enough.

I couldn't breathe. My throat was closing up. The phantom hands were back. Squeezing.

Patricia was talking. Something about the thirty-day window.

But all I could think about was Tyler's face in that hallway. The way he'd looked at me. The way he'd smiled. The way he'd smoothed his white shirt like he was reliving that night. Like he missed it.

Eventually, he was going to get access to Grace. And there was nothing I could do about it.

Tyler stood across the courtroom. Smoothed his white shirt one more time. Looked at me.

Smiled. That cold, predatory smile nobody else saw. Then walked out like he'd just won a business deal.

I made it to the parking lot before I started shaking so hard I couldn't stand.

Linda held me up. Actually held me.

"He looked at me." I grabbed Linda's arms. My fingers were probably leaving marks, but I couldn't let go. "In the hallway. When no one was watching. He looked at me like... like he wanted to do it again. Like he was enjoying this."

My other hand was at my throat. I couldn't stop touching it. Checking. Making sure his hands weren't there.

Linda's face went pale.

"Did anyone else see?"

"No. That's the point. He made sure no one saw."

"We'll tell Patricia. We'll—"

"Tell her what?" I dropped my hands. Forced them to my sides. "That he smiled at me? That he gave me a creepy look? That I felt his hands on my throat even though he was twenty feet away?"

I laughed. It came out broken. Desperate.

"They'll say I'm hysterical. Paranoid. Making things up."

Linda didn't argue.

Because she knew I was right.

Life doesn't stop breaking you just because you're already broken.

Two weeks after the custody hearing, Grace had her appointment with the neurologist. Her pediatrician had recommended it after a couple of examinations. Grace was small, really small, and not hitting her milestones like other babies.

The neurologist appointment was the following week.

I know because I stared at that date on my calendar and circled it in red pen, like marking a death sentence.

Grace was eight months old. Maybe she'd catch up. Maybe the drinking hadn't hurt her as badly as I feared.

But Linda kept pushing. Kept saying we needed answers. And I knew. Deep down, I knew what the answers would be. I just didn't want to hear them out loud.

Dr. Wilson's office smelled like hand sanitizer and something else. Something sterile and cold that made my stomach turn.

Antiseptic. The sharp alcohol smell that signifies doctors and needles and bad news.

Mixed with something else. Fear. Other parents who'd received bad news in these same rooms.

The waiting room had toys in the corner. Bright plastic things. A fish tank bubbling in the wall. Supposed to be calming.

It wasn't.

Dr. Wilson was younger than I expected. Maybe forty. Dark hair pulled back. Kind eyes. But the kind of kind that suggests she's about to tell you something terrible.

The appointment took two hours. Two hours of hell disguised as a medical evaluation.

Dr. Wilson's office was small. Harsh lights overhead that buzzed. An exam table covered in crinkly paper. Posters on the walls showing brain development. Developmental milestone charts.

Each milestone Grace couldn't meet.

She asked a million questions. Her voice was calm. Professional. As if she were asking about the weather and not about how I destroyed my daughter.

"Tell me about your pregnancy."

"Were you drinking?"

"How much?"

"When did you stop?"

I answered everything. My voice sounded distant, as if someone else was talking. As if I was floating above my own body again.

I watched her write it all down, observed her pen move across the paper. Blue ink on white forms. Scratch scratch scratch.

Each word felt like a nail going into a coffin. I watched her face remain carefully neutral. Professional. Practiced. The expression doctors wear when they already know what's wrong but have to conduct the full evaluation anyway.

She knew. She already knew. The questions were just confirmation. Documentation. Evidence.

Then came the tests. That's when I started to break.

Dr. Wilson placed Grace on a mat on the floor. A soft blue mat with alphabet letters on it. Bright. Cheerful. Educational.

Grace smiled at her. My daughter has the best smile. It lights up her whole face and makes her look like she knows a secret.

For a moment, she looked perfect. Normal. Like nothing was wrong.

"Can you sit up for me, sweetheart?"

Grace tried. God, she tried so hard.

She pushed herself up, her little arms shaking with the effort. Muscles straining. Her face flushed. Veins visible in her temples.

She fell over. Soft thump. Dr. Wilson sat her up again. Gentle. Patient.

"Try again, Grace. You can do it."

Grace tried again. Pushing. Straining. Her breath coming faster.

She fell again.

My chest tightened. Like someone was sitting on it. Like I couldn't get enough air. The room felt smaller. Hotter. The walls pressing in.

Dr. Wilson grabbed a bright red toy. Some kind of rattle that made noise. She moved it slowly in front of Grace's face. Left to right. Watching Grace's eyes.

Grace's eyes followed it, tracking the movement. But slowly. As if she were moving through water. As if everything was harder for her than it should be. As if the signals from her brain to her eyes took too long to arrive.

The toy made a sound. A gentle jingle. Nothing loud. Nothing scary. Grace startled. Her whole body jerked. Arms flying out. Face crumpling.

She started to cry. Not just fussy crying. Scared crying. Overwhelmed crying. The kind that says the world is too much and everything hurts.

"It's okay, baby." I was halfway out of my chair. "It's okay."

Dr. Wilson picked her up and handed her to me.

Grace buried her face in my neck, still crying, still scared of a toy that any other baby would have just laughed at or tried to grab.

Her hot breath against my skin, her tears soaking through my shirt collar. The room smelled like fear, like failure, like vodka, even though there was none.

More tests, each one worse than the last.

Dr. Wilson watched everything, taking notes on her clipboard, pen scratching. Her face was kind but unreadable. Professional distance. The face doctors wear when they're documenting tragedy.

I sat in the corner of the room in a plastic chair that was too small, meant for children, answering questions when asked, watching my daughter fail every single test, knowing it was my fault. The words kept echoing in my head, the questions from earlier.

Were you drinking? How much? How often?

Every drink I'd had before I knew she existed, every night I'd drowned in vodka, every morning I'd woken up shaking and poured more.

All of it sat before me now: eight months old and broken because of me.

Finally, Dr. Wilson sat down across from me, pulling her chair close. The wheels squeaked against the linoleum as she looked me in the eye.

Her eyes were kind, which made it worse somehow. I wanted her to be angry, to yell at me, to tell me I was a monster who poisoned her own daughter.

Instead, she was kind. Professional kindness. The worst kind.

"Your daughter has FASD. It stands for Fetal Alcohol Spectrum Disorder."

The words just kind of... floated there, hanging in the air like smoke, as if they were in a different language. My brain couldn't process them, couldn't grab onto them and make them real.

"Your drinking during early pregnancy caused neurological damage." Her voice was still gentle, still kind. "It's affecting her development."

Now the words landed. Now they hit. Like getting punched in the stomach. Like drowning. Like the room was shrinking, and I couldn't breathe, and everything was ending.

The walls pressed closer. The air thickened. My vision tunneled.

I did this. I poisoned my own daughter.

Dr. Wilson kept talking. I heard some of it. Most of it just washed over me like noise. Like being underwater. Sounds that didn't make sense.

"She will face challenges. Motor skills. Speech. Cognition. Sensory processing."

Each word was another punch.

"Learning disabilities. Behavioral issues. Impulse control problems. Social difficulties."

Each diagnosis was another thing I'd stolen from her. Another piece of normal I'd destroyed.

"But." Dr. Wilson leaned forward, as if she were trying to will me to listen, to pull me back from wherever I was drowning. "But with support and therapy, she can thrive. Children with FASD can have good lives. They just need more support than other children. More patience. More understanding."

I couldn't speak. Couldn't breathe. Couldn't do any-thing but sit there with Grace in my lap. Feeling her weight against my chest. Feeling her breathe. Warm and alive and broken.

Knowing I'd broken her before she even had a chance.

"This isn't a death sentence," Dr. Wilson said. Her voice was firm now. Strong. Like she was trying to grab me through the fog. "With early intervention, Grace can have a full life. She'll just need help getting there. And you're here. You're getting her help. That's what matters now."

"I did this."

My voice cracked. Broke into a thousand pieces. The words scraped out of my throat like broken glass.

"I poisoned my own daughter."

The words tasted like ash in my mouth. Like dirt. Like rot. Like vodka I hadn't touched in over a year but that still haunted everything.

Dr. Wilson's face softened. She reached out and put her hand on my knee. Warm. Solid. Real.

"You had an addiction. You got help. You got sober. That matters. You showing up now matters. You're here. You're asking for help. That's what Grace needs."

But Grace would never be whole. Would never be what she could have been. Because I chose vodka over her health before I even knew she existed.

The cycle I'd promised to break. I'd broken it by breaking her instead.

When I got home, I was still in the driver's seat. I put my hands on the wheel. The steering wheel was hot from the sun. It burned my palms.

I couldn't move. I couldn't make myself get out of the car. I couldn't make myself tell Linda what the doctor said.

The sobs came from somewhere deep. Somewhere I didn't know existed. They ripped out of me. Violent and real. Animal sounds. Like Grace's sounds. Like neither of us had words for this.

Grace didn't understand. Thank God she didn't understand. Thank God she didn't know what I'd done to her. What I'd stolen before she even had a chance.

Linda found me in the driveway an hour later. Still sitting in the car, still crying. My face swollen, eyes burning, throat raw.

Grace was asleep now, exhausted from the appointment, from trying so hard and failing every test.

Linda opened my door. She didn't say anything at first; just crouched down so she was eye level with me. Her knees cracked. She was getting older. We both were.

"Come inside, baby."

"I can't."

"Yes, you can."

"I destroyed her." My voice was raw. Broken. Barely a whisper. "I destroyed my own daughter."

Linda's face was firm, strong. She didn't look away, didn't flinch, didn't let me hide.

"You made mistakes. You have an addiction." She put her hand on my knee. Warm. Solid. Real. "And you got sober to protect her. Now you show up for her: every therapy appointment, every doctor visit, every single day."

"It's not enough." Fresh tears were running down my face, hot and fast. "It's not enough to fix what I did."

"It's what you've got." Linda squeezed my knee harder. "So it has to be enough."

She was right.

What else could I do? Drown in guilt? Start drinking again? Give up? Grace deserved better than a mother who gave up, even if that mother had broken her before she was born.

Chapter Six

The Interview

T HERAPY STARTED THE FOLLOWING week.

Grace was nine months old now. She still couldn't sit up by herself. She couldn't crawl. She could barely hold a toy.

The gaps were widening. Other babies were pulling themselves up on furniture and cruising. Some were even walking.

Grace couldn't sit. But God, she was trying. I watched her in physical therapy, her face red from effort, her little arms shaking as she tried to push herself up on all fours.

The mat beneath her was soft, blue, safe.

Falling.

The therapist was patient, a young woman with a ponytail and kind eyes. "Good job, Grace! Try again!" Grace made a sound, a grunt of frustration, of anger at her own body for not working right.

But she tried again, pushing, straining, her face determined. Falling. Trying. Falling. Trying.

My chest hurt watching her, but not in a bad way anymore.

A different kind. The kind that comes from seeing someone fight even when they don't realize they're fighting, when they don't know they're behind, when they just know they want something and keep trying until they get it.

That's when I realized something.

Grace was a fighter.

She didn't know she was delayed. She didn't know other babies her age were crawling, sitting, and babbling actual words. She just knew she wanted to move, and she kept trying.

If she could keep trying, so could I.

I couldn't fix what I'd done. I couldn't go back in time and not drink. I couldn't give her the brain she should've had.

But I could show up. Every time she fell down, I could be there to help her try again.

That night, I sat in Linda's guest room, Grace asleep in her crib beside my bed. The room smelled like baby powder and the lavender lotion Linda used.

My business was dying. Grace was delayed. Everything was falling apart. And I had no way to stop Tyler from taking her.

No way to prove he was still dangerous, that the therapy and treatment were just a mask. No way to fight someone with Margaret Carrington's money and power.

I opened my nightstand drawer. The wood stuck a little; it needed oil. Inside were the things I'd kept from the worst times. Things I couldn't throw away but couldn't look at either.

The hospital bracelet from Grace's birth, her first footprints on thick paper, and the surgery consent form I'd signed.

And a business card, slightly bent, its corner dog-eared from being carried in my pocket for months before I finally put it in the drawer.

Elena RodriguezInvestigative ReporterChicago Tribune

A phone number written in pen on the back. Personal cell. Not the office line.

She'd given it to me months ago, after my video went viral, after I raised the money for Grace's surgery, after strangers donated $180,000 to save my daughter's life.

"If you ever want to tell your full story," she'd said, "call me. Anytime."

I'd said no then. Too scared, too raw, too worried about making things worse.

I'd kept the card anyway, hidden in this drawer where I wouldn't have to look at it, where I wouldn't be tempted.

I held it now. The paper was soft from handling, from the months I'd carried it before putting it away.

My phone sat on the nightstand, charging, the screen dark.

I looked at Grace, her chest rising and falling, the scar from her heart surgery barely visible in the dim light, her hands curled into little fists, fighting even in her sleep.

I thought about her in therapy today. Falling. Trying again. That determined look on her face, that grunt of frustration when her body wouldn't do what she wanted.

But she kept trying. She didn't give up. She didn't know how. If she could keep fighting, so could I.

I picked up my phone; the screen lit up, too bright in the dark room. I stared at Elena's number on the business card, thinking about Tyler, about Margaret, about the smear campaign destroying everything I'd built, about the custody petition coming, about handing Grace to her rapist father every week for the rest of her childhood.

I dialed. It rang once, twice, three times. Maybe she wouldn't answer. Maybe it was too late. Maybe—

"Hello?"

Elena's voice: alert, professional, not sleepy even though it was almost midnight.

"Elena Rodriguez?"

"Yes. Who's this?"

"It's Olivia Parker."

Silence. Just for a beat.

"Olivia?" Her voice changed, warmer, more careful. "I'm glad you called. What can I do for you?"

My throat was tight. The words stuck. Grace made a small sound in her sleep. Not quite a cry, just a murmur.

I looked at her, at my daughter who had already survived so much: heart surgery, NICU, delays she'd fight her whole life. She deserved better than a mother who stayed silent out of fear.

"I want to do the interview," I said. The words came out rough, raw. "I want to tell my story. About Tyler Carrington. About what he did to me."

"Okay." Elena's voice was steady, not excited, not pushing, just... there. "Can I ask what changed your mind?"

I looked at Grace again.

"Tyler's lawyers are filing for custody. He may get visitation rights soon. Maybe more. And I can't... I can't just hand my daughter to him without fighting back."

My voice cracked.

"Even if I lose. Even if this makes everything worse. I have to try."

"Olivia." Elena's voice was gentle. "You understand what this means? The Carringtons will come after you. Hard. They have resources we can't match."

"I know."

"This could destroy what's left of your business, your reputation, everything you've built."

"It's already destroying it." I wiped my eyes with the back of my hand. "Margaret's been running a smear campaign for months: anonymous articles calling me an exploiter. My platform's dying. I'm barely making rent."

Silence on the line.

"So what do I have left to lose?"

"Your sobriety," Elena said quietly. "Your daughter. Your sanity."

The words hung there. Heavy. True.

"Maybe." I pulled my knees up to my chest. The phone pressed hard against my ear. "But I will still do it. I need to let everyone know that Tyler's a serial predator."

"Okay."

I heard Elena moving on the other end, papers rustling, as if she was already taking notes.

"I need to be honest with you," she said.

"This is going to be hard. The hardest thing you've ever done. I'll need documentation: medical records, police reports, everything. And I'll need you to go on record. Your name. Your face. No hiding."

My stomach turned.

"And Tyler's lawyers will tear you apart. They'll bring up your prostitution. Your homelessness. Your drinking. Everything you've ever done that they can use against you."

"I know."

"And the Carringtons might still win. Money usually does."

"I know that too." Grace stirred in her crib and made another small sound. I reached over, put my hand on her chest, and felt her heartbeat. Strong. Fixed. Fighting.

"But I have to try," I whispered. "She's a fighter, my daughter. She tries every day, even though everything's harder for her, even though her own body won't work right. She keeps trying."

My voice broke.

"If she can keep fighting, so can I."

Silence on the line, just breathing. Then Elena's voice, soft but firm:

"Okay. We'll do this. But we do it right, carefully, with every piece of evidence we can find."

"When?"

"Tomorrow. Can I come to you at ten AM?"

Tomorrow. Twelve hours away. Twelve hours to change my mind, to back out, to stay silent and safe.

"Yes," I said, before I could think about it, before fear could stop me. "Tomorrow."

"Thank you for your courage, Olivia."

Courage. I didn't feel courageous. I felt terrified.

But I looked at Grace, at her little chest rising and falling, at the scar from her heart surgery, at her hands curled into fists even in sleep, at my daughter who fought every day just to do things other babies did naturally.

"Thank you," I whispered. I hung up and sat there in the dark with the phone in my hand and the business card on my lap.

Knowing I'd just started a war I might not win. Knowing the Carringtons would destroy me for this. Knowing I might lose everything.

I whispered to Grace in the darkness, "I'm going to fight for you, even if I lose, even if it costs everything."

Grace made a small sound. Not a word, just a sound. But it was enough. Tomorrow, I'd tell my truth and hope someone was listening.

Maybe the truth was a weapon after all, even if it was the only one I had left.

Elena Rodriguez sat at Linda's kitchen table. She looked younger than the first time I saw her after the viral video. Maybe thirty, with dark hair pulled back and kind but sharp eyes, like she saw everything.

"Thank you for agreeing to this," she said. "I know it's not easy."

"It's necessary." My voice was steadier than I felt. "Tyler Carrington is trying to get custody of my daughter. The court thinks he's reformed. But he's not. He's still dangerous. And no one will believe me unless I tell the truth. All of it."

Elena pulled out a recording device. "Tell me everything. Start from the beginning."

So I did. I told her everything. About the Peninsula Hotel meltdown, the prostitution, the drugged wine, the dark room with Bach playing and that pine smell. About waking up with hours missing, bruises around my wrists and neck, the rape kit that matched Tyler's DNA. About the prosecutor who believed me but couldn't file charges, Margaret's smear campaign, the settlement I refused to sign, and Tyler's cold smile in the courthouse hallway.

I told her everything. Elena listened, took notes, and asked questions.

"Do you have documentation? Medical records? Police reports?"

"Everything. I kept everything."

"I mentioned this over the phone yesterday, but I want to make sure you understand what you are getting into. Are you prepared for the backlash? The Carringtons will come after you. Hard."

"I know. I need to do this because Tyler's trying to take Grace. And I'm not letting that happen without a fight."

The interview took four hours. When it was over, Elena packed up her recorder.

"This will publish in two weeks. I need time to fact-check, contact Tyler's lawyers for comment, and build the full story."

"Will it make a difference?"

"I don't know." Elena's voice was honest, gentle. "But I believe you. And I think other people will too."

"And if they don't?"

"Then at least you told the truth. At least you fought."

She left. I sat at the table, exhausted, terrified, but also something else. Lighter. Like I'd been carrying something heavy and finally put it down. The truth was out there now.

Soon, everyone would know. And maybe... just maybe... Tyler wouldn't get away with it this time. Maybe people would know that Tyler Carrington was a predator who belonged in prison, not in a courtroom fighting for custody of the daughter he conceived by raping me.

The article was published on a Tuesday morning.

I sat in Linda's living room with my phone in my lap, refreshing the Chicago Tribune website every thirty seconds as if it would change anything.

There it was. Front page of the online edition.

"The Carrington Assault: One Woman's Account of Rape, Retaliation, and the System That Failed Her"

By Elena Rodriguez

My stomach dropped. My hands went cold.

It was real now. Out there. Everyone could see it.

I read it three times. Elena had done exactly what she promised. Every detail. Every piece of evidence. The rape kit. The DNA match. Dana Whitaker's statement about why she couldn't prosecute. Margaret's settlement offers. The smear campaign.

My whole life laid out in 5,000 words.

Grace was on a blanket on the floor, playing with her toes. Nine months old, and she had no idea her mother had just set everything on fire.

I waited for something to happen.

Nothing did. In the first hour, seventeen people shared it on Twitter. I counted each one.

By lunch, maybe two hundred shares. A few comments. Most of them called me a liar. A gold digger. A whore looking for a payday.

By dinner, the article had dropped off the Tribune's front page, replaced by something about the mayor's budget proposal.

I sat there holding Grace, watching the sun go down through Linda's kitchen window.

That was it. I'd told the truth. Put everything on the line. And nobody cared.

The hate started that night. My phone buzzed. Once. Then again. Then it didn't stop buzzing.

Someone had posted my video. The one I'd recorded in Linda's bathroom four months ago. The raw, broken confession I'd made when I thought nobody would ever see it.

I watched it blow up in real time. But not the way I'd hoped. The comments rolled in like a flood. Hundreds of them. Then thousands.

She's lying for attention

Gold digger trying to get money from a billionaire

Why would he rape HER?

Another false accusation destroying a man's life

She was a prostitute; what did she expect?

I read every single one. I couldn't stop myself. Each comment was a punch to the stomach, but I kept scrolling. Kept reading. Kept bleeding.

Samantha called. "Stop looking at your phone. Right now."

"They don't believe me."

"Some people never will. You knew that going in."

"But I told the truth. Elena laid out all the evidence—"

"The truth doesn't matter to people who've already made up their minds." Her voice was gentle but firm. "Put your phone down. Take care of Grace. This will pass."

But it didn't pass. It got worse.

By Wednesday morning, Carrington Media was in full defense mode.

I woke up to notifications. Hundreds of them. New articles. Video segments. Social media posts. All from Carrington outlets or their partners.

"False Accusations: The Disturbing Pattern of Women Targeting Wealthy Men" - Carrington News Network

"Tyler Carrington's Mother Speaks Out Against 'Baseless Smear Campaign'" - The Financial Post

"Investigative Report Reveals Inconsistencies in Parker Claims" - Carrington Daily

They had everything ready, as if they'd been waiting for this. Planning for it.

Margaret's statement played on loop across every Carrington channel:

"These recycled allegations have been thoroughly investigated by law enforcement and found to be without merit. Ms. Parker's continued obsession with my family is deeply troubling. We considered this matter closed months ago. Her decision to resurrect these false claims, coinciding with a custody dispute, speaks to her true motivations."

Tyler's lawyers issued their own statement:

"Our client categorically denies these allegations. The Cook County District Attorney's Office conducted a thorough investigation and declined to file charges. Ms. Parker has a documented history of substance abuse, prostitution, and making false statements. This is nothing more than a calculated attempt to extort money and damage our client's reputation."

Calculated. Extort. False statements. The words stabbed.

I sat on Linda's couch and watched myself get destroyed on live television.

A legal analyst on Carrington News: *"The timing is very suspicious. Ms. Parker only came forward publicly after Mr. Carrington filed for custody of his daughter. That suggests this may be more about parental rights than actual assault."*

A women's advocate on the same network: *"We have to be careful about believing every allegation, especially when there's clear financial motivation. The Carringtons are billionaires. That makes them targets for this kind of accusation."*

They made it look balanced. Two sides. Just asking questions. But the questions were designed to make me look like a liar.

By Thursday, my subscriber count had dropped another eight thousand, down to 61,000 now. Hemorrhaging followers like blood from a wound.

The comments on my channel were a war zone.

Lost all respect for you.

Using your daughter for views is disgusting.

This is why no one believes women anymore.

But there were other comments too. Smaller. Quieter. Easy to miss in the flood of hate.

I believe you.

Thank you for being brave.

This happened to me too.

I held onto those comments like life rafts.

Grace needed a diaper change. A bottle. A nap. She didn't care about Twitter or cable news or subscriber counts. She just needed her mom.

I put my phone in a drawer and didn't look at it for six hours.

Saturday morning, my phone rang.

Unknown number. I almost didn't answer. I had been ignoring most calls. Too many reporters. Too many people with opinions about my rape.

But something made me pick up.

"Is this Olivia Parker?" A woman's voice. Young. Trembling.

"Yes."

"My name is Amanda Lopez. I... I read your article. And I need to tell you something."

My whole body went still.

"Tyler Carrington raped me too."

The words hung in the air. I couldn't breathe.

"When?"

"Three years ago. I was a senior at Northeastern. He was a year ahead of me." Her voice cracked. "I've never told anyone. Not the police. Not my family. Nobody."

"Amanda—"

"Can I talk to the journalist? The one who wrote your article? I want to tell my story."

My heart was beating. Grace stirred against my chest.

"Yes. Yes, I'll give you her number."

"Thank you." Amanda was crying now. "Thank you for being brave. I thought I was the only one."

After we hung up, I sat there for a long time.

I wasn't alone. Tyler had done this before. I called Elena immediately.

Amanda's story published Tuesday.

"'He Said I Drank Too Much': Second Woman Accuses Tyler Carrington of Rape."

She'd been twenty-one. Tyler invited her to dinner. Wine at his apartment afterward. She remembered feeling dizzy. Then nothing. Hours missing. Waking up in his bed, clothes disheveled, body aching.

Tyler was apologetic: "You had too much to drink. I made sure you were safe."

But Amanda knew. The way I'd known. Something happened in those missing hours. She never reported it. Tyler graduated. Moved back to Chicago. Started working for his mother.

Amanda spent three years thinking she was crazy. Making it up. That she had really just drunk too much. Until she read my article. The response was different this time.

Not hate. Not immediately. People were listening.

Wednesday afternoon, another email came through Elena's website.

Subject: "Tyler Carrington raped me"

A woman named Sarah Mitchell. Boston College. Two years ago.

Same story. Dinner. Wine. Missing hours. Waking up knowing something terrible had happened but having no proof.

Tyler's apology: "We both had too much to drink. Things got out of hand."

Sarah told her roommate. Her roommate suggested maybe Tyler was telling the truth. Maybe they both just drank too much. So Sarah stayed quiet. Until now.

Thursday, a third woman came forward.

Jessica Ramirez. Northwestern grad. Tyler's year. Same fraternity parties where he'd likely started perfecting his technique.

Drugged drink. Missing hours. Waking up in his room.

"You don't remember? Wow, you really can't handle your alcohol."

Three women. Three nearly identical stories.

Elena published all three together.

"A Pattern of Predation: Three More Women Accuse Tyler Carrington of Sexual Assault"

The article went viral in hours. Not thousands of shares. Hundreds of thousands. Every major outlet picked it up: CNN, MSNBC, ABC, and Fox News.

The comments shifted dramatically.

One woman can be lying. Four women with identical stories? No way.

This is what predators do. They find a method that works and repeat it.

Tyler Carrington belongs in prison.

Carrington Media tried to fight back. But their counter-campaign looked weak now. Desperate.

Margaret's new statement: "These coordinated allegations are part of a calculated attack on our family."

But nobody was buying it anymore. Four women. Four identical patterns. Four rapes that Tyler thought he'd gotten away with.

Friday morning, Detective Smith called.

"Olivia. The Cook County DA's office is reopening the investigation."

I almost dropped the phone.

"What?"

"Three new victims. All credible. All with similar accounts. The prosecutor who declined your case initially? She's willing to take another look."

"They're filing charges?"

"Not yet. But they're investigating. Formally. That's a start."

My legs gave out. I sat down hard on Linda's kitchen floor.

Grace crawled over, pulled herself up on my shoulder, and patted my wet cheeks with her tiny hands.

"What happens now?" I asked Smith.

"We investigate. Interview all four women. Re-examine evidence. Build a case." He paused. "Tyler's lawyers will fight. But with four women? Same pattern? This is different."

After he hung up, I sat on the floor and cried. Not sad crying. Not scared crying. Relief. The kind that comes after holding your breath for so long that you forget what air tastes like.

Grace climbed into my lap and wrapped her arms around my neck. I held my daughter and let myself feel something I hadn't felt in months.

Hope.

The hearing was scheduled for Monday morning. Emergency custody modification. Judge Foster's courtroom. 9 AM.

Tyler's lawyers tried to block it, filing three motions arguing that the criminal investigation shouldn't impact civil custody proceedings.

Judge Foster denied all three.

Patricia called Sunday night with the news.

"The judge wants to hear from both sides about the criminal investigation. She's considering suspending Tyler's visitation pending the outcome."

"Suspending?" My voice came out small, fearful of hope.

"If she thinks Grace might be in danger, she can suspend his rights temporarily until the criminal case is resolved."

"Do you think she will?"

"Four women, Olivia. Four credible allegations of rape using the same method. Tyler drugged and raped four women that we know about." Patricia's voice was firm. "Yes. I think she will."

That night, I couldn't sleep. I lay in Linda's guest room with Grace in her crib beside me, listening to her breathe and watching her chest rise and fall in the dark.

Monday morning, Judge Foster's courtroom was packed. Press in the back rows. Tyler and his legal team on one side. Me and Patricia on the other.

Margaret Carrington sat behind Tyler, perfectly composed in a designer suit, not a hair out of place.

But I saw it. The crack in her armor. The way her jaw was too tight. Her hands gripping her purse as if she might strangle it.

Tyler looked worse. Pale, with sweat on his forehead despite the cold courtroom.

Good. Let him sweat.

Judge Foster entered. We all stood. She didn't waste time.

"I've reviewed the recent developments in the criminal investigation involving Mr. Carrington. Four women have now come forward with remarkably similar allegations of sexual assault. The Cook County District Attorney has formally reopened the case."

Tyler's lawyer stood. "Your Honor, these allegations have no bearing on—"

"Sit down, Mr. Sterling." Judge Foster's voice could cut glass. "I'm not finished."

He sat.

"This court's primary concern is the welfare of the minor child. When credible allegations suggest a parent may pose a danger—"

"These allegations are not credible," Sterling interrupted. "They're coordinated. Calculated. Part of a clear pattern of—"

"Mr. Sterling. I will hold you in contempt if you interrupt me again."

Silence.

Judge Foster looked at Tyler. Really looked at him. The way she'd looked at me in our first hearing. Seeing. Judging.

"Four women. Four nearly identical accounts. A documented pattern of predatory behavior." She paused. "Until the criminal investigation is complete, I am suspending Mr. Carrington's visitation rights with the minor child."

The courtroom erupted.

Tyler's lawyers were on their feet, objecting. Margaret's hand was on Tyler's arm, gripping tight. Reporters were scribbling notes.

I sat there unable to move. Suspended. Grace was safe.

"This is a temporary order," Judge Foster continued over the noise. "If Mr. Carrington is cleared of all charges, we will revisit custody arrangements. But until then, the child remains in Ms. Parker's sole custody."

Her gavel came down. It was over.

Tyler turned to look at me across the courtroom. No smile this time. Just rage. Pure, undiluted rage.

Margaret stood, leaned close to her son, and whispered something. Tyler's expression shifted. Calculated. Cold.

This wasn't over for them. They were already planning. Already strategizing. But right now, in this moment, I'd won. Grace was safe. And Tyler Carrington was finally facing consequences.

Patricia squeezed my hand. "You did it."

"We did it," I corrected.

But really, Amanda did it. Sarah did it. Jessica did it.

Four women who found the courage to speak up. Four women who saved my daughter.

Outside the courthouse, reporters swarmed. Cameras. Microphones. Questions shouted from every direction.

I stood on those steps holding Patricia's hand and faced them.

"I want to thank Amanda Lopez, Sarah Mitchell, and Jessica Ramirez for their incredible courage," I said into the cameras. "They didn't have to come forward. But they did. And because of them, my daughter is safe tonight."

More questions. More shouting. But I was done. I walked down those courthouse steps, got in Patricia's car, and went home to my daughter.

Grace was at Linda's, sitting on a blanket on the living room floor with blocks scattered around her. She looked up when I walked in, smiled, and reached for me.

I scooped her up, held her tight, and breathed in the smell of her hair.

"You're safe, baby girl. You're safe."

Linda was crying, watching us from the kitchen doorway.

"Is it really over?"

"No." I kissed Grace's head. "But we won today. That's enough."

That night, I sat in Grace's room while she slept. I watched her breathe in the dark, this perfect, innocent child who existed because of the worst thing that ever happened to me.

My phone buzzed. A text from Amanda: *Thank you for going first. I couldn't have done it without you.*

Then Sarah: *We're stronger together.*

Then Jessica: *He doesn't get to win anymore.*

Four women, four separate stories that were really the same story.

Tyler Carrington had spent years perfecting his method, choosing victims he thought wouldn't be believed: women who were alone, young, and easy to discredit.

He'd gotten away with it because predators usually do. But not this time. This time, we'd found each other, told the truth, and someone listened.

Chapter Seven

Blood Money

THE CALL CAME TWO weeks after the courthouse victory.

Patricia's number. Thursday morning. Grace was down for her nap, and I was folding laundry as if my life were normal.

"Margaret Carrington wants to meet."

My hands went cold. The tiny onesie I was holding fell to the floor.

"About what?"

"She wouldn't say. Just that she wants to discuss 'a resolution that benefits everyone involved.'" Patricia's voice was careful, the way people talk when they're trying not to scare you. "Her lawyers called this morning. Very formal. Very proper."

I sat down on Linda's couch. My legs had stopped working.

"You don't have to go," Patricia said. "You can say no."

"Will you be there?"

"Yes. And I've already told them. Anything they want to discuss goes through me first. Nothing happens without your approval."

"When?"

"Tomorrow. 2 PM. Sterling & Katz downtown."

The law firm that had filed fifty-three pages of motions before the DA even had DNA results. The firm with six lawyers on retainer just to keep Tyler out of prison.

I thought about hanging up, saying no, pretending I never got the call. But Margaret Carrington didn't do anything without a reason, and I needed to know what that reason was.

"I'll be there."

That night I couldn't sleep.

I lay in bed staring at the ceiling, listening to Grace breathe through the baby monitor. Every few minutes she'd make this soft sound. Not quite a snore, not quite a sigh. The sound of a baby who felt safe.

What does Margaret want?

Nothing good. That much I knew.

Tyler's visitation was suspended. The criminal investigation was moving forward. Four women had come forward with identical stories.

We were winning. Finally. So why did I feel like I was about to lose everything?

Sterling & Katz occupied the top three floors of a building that looked like it swallowed smaller buildings for breakfast.

The lobby was all marble and chrome and windows that seemed to stretch forever. A security desk with two guards checked my ID as if I might be carrying a bomb.

Patricia met me at the elevator bank. She wore her court suit, the expensive one she saved for cases she needed to win.

"Remember," she said as we rode up, "you don't have to agree to anything. We can walk out at any time. The second you're uncomfortable, we leave."

"What do you think she wants?"

"I don't know." Patricia watched the floor numbers climb. "But Margaret Carrington doesn't do anything without a strategy. Whatever she's offering, there's a catch."

The elevator stopped on 47. The doors opened onto more marble, more glass, views of Chicago that made the whole city look small, conquerable, like something you could own if you had enough money.

A receptionist in a suit that probably cost more than my car led us down a hallway. Her heels clicked on the marble. Each step was perfectly measured, perfectly controlled.

We stopped at a door. Conference Room A. The receptionist opened it.

And my stomach dropped.

Margaret sat at the head of a table that could seat twenty people.

Perfect gray suit. Perfect hair. Not a wrinkle, not a strand out of place. She looked like she'd been carved from ice.

Three men in expensive suits sat beside her. Lawyers. Tyler's legal team. I recognized one from the courthouse, the older guy with silver hair who'd tried to argue that four women with identical rape stories was just a coincidence.

But it was the other side of the table that made me stop breathing.

Amanda. Sarah. Jessica.

The other women. The other survivors. All three of them already sitting there, waiting. None of them had told me they'd be here.

Amanda looked up when I walked in. Her eyes were red and swollen, like she'd been crying for hours. Sarah wouldn't meet my gaze, just stared at her hands folded on the table.

Jessica looked exhausted, the kind of tired that goes bone-deep, that comes from fighting too long with nothing left.

"Ms. Parker. Good to see you again." Margaret's voice was pleasant, professional, as if we were here to discuss a business merger, not the fact that her son raped four women. "Thank you for coming. Please, sit."

Patricia pulled out a chair. I sat.

My heart was pounding so hard I could feel it in my throat.

"I'll get straight to the point," Margaret said. "This situation has become untenable for everyone involved."

She folded her hands on the table, looked at each of us in turn.

"My son's reputation has been damaged by allegations that cannot be proven. You four have been subjected to intense public scrutiny and harassment. The legal process will drag on for years with no guaranteed outcome. Everyone loses."

"Your son raped us!" I yelled.

The words came out before I realized it. It didn't sound like my voice.

"That's not an allegation. That's a fact."

The silver-haired lawyer, whose nameplate said Richard Sterling, opened a folder.

"The Cook County District Attorney has reopened the investigation but has not filed charges. To proceed to trial, they would need full cooperation from all alleged victims. Without that cooperation, they have no case."

He pulled out papers and slid them across the polished table.

"That leaves us with two paths forward. Path one: years of contentious litigation. Criminal proceedings. Civil suits. Discovery. Depositions. Trial. Your names and faces in the media for years. Your trauma relived over and over. And at the end, maybe a conviction. Maybe not. Juries are unpredictable."

He paused, letting that sink in.

"Path two: private resolution. Clean. Final. Allows everyone to move forward with their lives."

"You mean buying our silence," I said.

"I mean resolving legitimate civil claims."

Sterling pulled out four more folders, identical. He placed one in front of each of us.

I didn't open mine. Amanda did. Her hands were shaking so badly the pages rattled.

I watched her eyes move down the first page, saw them stop, and noticed her whole body go still.

"Two million dollars," Sterling said. "Per plaintiff. To resolve all potential civil claims related to the media coverage and reputational damage. Standard non-disclosure agreements. Standard release of liability."

The room went silent.

Two million dollars.

I heard Amanda make a small sound. Not quite a gasp, not quite a sob.

Sarah's hands went to her mouth.

Jessica just stared at the number like it might disappear if she looked away.

"What about the criminal case?" Patricia asked. Her voice was sharp, lawyer voice. She wasn't buying this.

"That's entirely separate," Sterling said carefully, each word measured, rehearsed. "What these women choose to do regarding their cooperation with prosecutors is, of course, their personal decision. We cannot and would not ask them to do anything improper."

The way he said it, so careful, so clean. He was asking us to do something improper. He just wasn't saying it out loud.

"Bullshit," I said. "You're paying us to disappear, to stop cooperating with the DA. That's witness tampering."

"This is a settlement of civil claims for defamation and emotional distress caused by media coverage." Sterling's voice didn't change. Still calm, still measured. "What you choose to do regarding your cooperation with law enforcement is entirely your own decision. Those are two separate matters."

"Except they're not separate at all."

"If you believe this constitutes witness tampering, you're welcome to report it to the authorities." Sterling smiled. It didn't reach his eyes. "But I assure you, we've been very careful about how this is structured. Every word of these contracts has been reviewed by multiple attorneys. This is a legitimate civil settlement. Nothing more."

He was right. I could feel it.

They'd found the loophole, the gray area, the place where legal and illegal blurred together just enough that they could get away with it.

Margaret finally spoke. Her voice was quiet, controlled, more terrifying than if she'd been shouting.

"Ms. Parker, I understand your position is unique. You have a daughter. You have an ongoing custody dispute with my son."

My chest tightened. Every muscle in my body tensed.

"If you accept this settlement, Tyler will permanently withdraw his custody petition. You will have sole legal and physical custody of Grace. Full custody. No visitation. No contact. He will sign away all parental rights. You and your daughter will never have to see him again."

The words hit like a physical blow.

Grace. Safe. Forever.

No more court hearings. No more lawyers arguing about supervised visits. No more fear that Tyler would show up at daycare. No more nightmares about losing her.

Just... over.

"That agreement will be legally binding and filed separately from this settlement," Margaret continued. "But it's contingent on your acceptance of these terms."

There it was. The hook. The thing I couldn't refuse.

Margaret paused. She looked at Sterling. He opened another folder.

"There's one additional provision for you, Olivia," she said. Her voice was casual, as if she were discussing the weather.

"Both you and your daughter will waive any and all claims to inheritance from Tyler Carrington, from myself, or from Carrington Media Group. In perpetuity."

The words took a second to land. Then I understood. This wasn't just about settling a lawsuit. This was about protecting their money.

Their billions.

Margaret was willing to pay $2 million. $8 million total for all four of us to ensure Grace could never claim a penny of the Carrington fortune.

Margaret and Tyler were probably worth hundreds of millions, if not billions. Carrington Media Group was an empire.

And they were spending $8 million to ensure my daughter, Tyler's biological daughter, would never touch any of it.

"You're buying us off," I said. My voice came out flat. Dead.

"I'm ensuring clarity," Margaret corrected. "Tyler is relinquishing his parental rights. That means your daughter has no legal relationship to him. This provision simply formalizes that she has no claim to his estate or mine."

"She's his daughter."

"No. No. Not after he signs these papers, she isn't. Legally, she'll be nothing to him. A stranger." Margaret's expression didn't change. "This protects everyone. You get certainty. Grace gets certainty. Tyler gets certainty. No one can come back later claiming they're owed something."

Sterling slid another document across the table.

"Standard estate waiver," he said. "Ms. Parker and the minor child waive all claims to inheritance, trust funds, or any other financial consideration from the Carrington family or associated entities. This includes any claims that might arise from the biological relationship or any other connection."

I stared at the paper.

Two million dollars now. For the promise that Grace would never get a penny more.

Margaret was protecting her empire. Making sure that in twenty years, thirty years, forty years, Grace couldn't show up claiming inheritance rights as Tyler's biological daughter.

Eight million dollars was nothing to the Carringtons. It was an insurance policy. Cheap at that price.

"And if we don't agree to this provision?" I asked.

"Then there's no settlement," Sterling said simply. "The custody withdrawal is contingent on your acceptance of all terms, including the estate waiver."

Of course it was. Margaret had thought of everything.

She wasn't just buying Tyler's freedom. She was buying her family's future. Making sure my daughter could never be a threat to the Carrington fortune.

"I need to speak with my clients," Patricia said. Her voice was tight. Angry. "Privately."

Margaret nodded. Stood. Her lawyers stood with her. Perfect synchronization. Like they'd practiced.

"Of course. Take your time."

They filed out. The door clicked shut behind them. And then it was just the four of us.

For a long moment, nobody spoke.

The five of us sat in that enormous conference room. The city sprawling below us through floor-to-ceiling windows. Chicago looked small and manageable from up here. From where the Carringtons lived.

Patricia spoke first. Her lawyer voice. Clear. Precise. Making sure we understood exactly what we were signing.

"Before anyone says anything, I need to make sure you all understand the legal terms you're agreeing to."

She pulled out her own copies of the contracts. Started going through them methodically.

"First, the terms that apply to all four of you." She looked at each of us in turn. "Two million dollars per plaintiff to settle civil claims related to defamation and emotional distress caused by the media coverage. In exchange, you sign non-disclosure agreements."

She flipped to a marked page.

"The NDAs prohibit you from discussing Tyler Carrington, the assault allegations, or this settlement. Ever. With anyone. You can't write about it. Can't talk about it in interviews. Can't post about it online. Can't discuss it with family members outside of the immediate household. Can't even mention it to therapists unless they sign their own NDA."

Patricia looked up.

"You sign this, and you can never tell your story again. As far as the public is concerned, this never happened. Any violation of the NDA subjects you to immediate repayment of the full settlement amount plus penalties. They've structured it so that if you speak out, you'll owe them more than they paid you."

She let that sink in.

"Second, the criminal case. None of you are legally obligated to cooperate with prosecution. As victims, you have the absolute right to decline participation. However—" She paused. "The Cook County DA cannot proceed without cooperative witnesses. If all four of you decline to testify, they will have no choice but to drop the charges."

"So Tyler walks free," Jessica said quietly.

"Yes. In practical terms, accepting this settlement means Tyler Carrington will face no criminal prosecution for any of the alleged assaults."

Amanda made a small sound. Like something breaking.

Patricia's voice softened slightly. But she kept going. We needed to hear this.

"Third, there's a unanimous acceptance requirement. All four plaintiffs must agree to the settlement. If even one person declines, the entire offer is withdrawn from everyone."

She looked at me when she said this.

"If Olivia says no, none of you get the money. If any of you say no, Olivia doesn't get the custody agreement. You're bound together by this structure. That's intentional. It's designed to create pressure."

Sarah was crying now. Quiet tears streaming down her face.

Patricia turned to me specifically.

"Olivia, your agreement includes two additional provisions that don't apply to the others. First, Tyler will permanently withdraw from all custody proceedings and relinquish all parental rights to Grace. You'll have sole legal and physical custody. No visitation. No contact. Forever."

My chest felt tight.

"Second, and this is critical. You and Grace will sign an estate waiver. You'll be waiving any and all claims to inheritance from Tyler, from Margaret, or from Carrington Media Group."

She pulled out the specific page. Made me look at it.

"Grace is Tyler's biological daughter. Even if he gives up parental rights, she has a potential legal claim to his estate when he dies. Tyler is worth an estimated $300 million. Margaret is worth approximately $1 billion. Carrington Media Group is valued at over $10 billion."

The numbers were so big they didn't feel real.

"This waiver means Grace will never be able to claim any of that. Not when Tyler dies. Not when Margaret dies. Not ever. In exchange, you're receiving $2 million now and Tyler's permanent absence from your lives."

Patricia looked at me directly.

"Margaret Carrington is paying you $2 million to ensure that Grace, who could potentially be entitled to hundreds of millions as Tyler's heir, never touches a penny of the Carrington fortune. She's paying $8 million total to protect billions. It's an extremely favorable deal for her."

"It's a bargain," I said. My voice sounded hollow. "She's buying us off cheap."

"Yes. That's exactly what this is." The room went silent again.

Patricia closed her folder.

"Those are the terms. Now you need to decide if you can live with them."

Nobody moved for a long time. Then Amanda put her face in her hands and started to sob. Not quiet crying. Full-body sobs that shook the table. Like something inside her had finally broken completely.

Sarah reached over and put her hand on Amanda's shoulder. She was crying too. Had been crying since Patricia started explaining the terms.

"I'm sorry," Amanda gasped through her hands. "I'm so sorry. But I can't do this anymore. I can't keep fighting."

She looked up. Her face was destroyed. Red, blotchy, and wet.

"I have $180,000 in student loans. I'm working sixty hours a week at two jobs, and I still can't make rent some months. I'm drowning, Olivia. I'm actually drowning."

She wiped her eyes with the back of her hand, but the tears kept coming.

"My parents are immigrants. They came here with nothing. They've worked minimum wage their entire lives, and they're still barely surviving. This money—" Her voice broke. "This money would change everything. I could pay off my loans. Help my parents finally breathe. Maybe go back to school. Maybe have a life that isn't just work and debt and panic."

She put her head back in her hands.

"I know it's wrong. I know we're letting him win. But I'm so tired. I'm so fucking tired."

Sarah spoke next. Her voice was barely a whisper.

"My mom has stage four cancer." The words hung in the air like smoke.

"Eight months of treatment. Surgery. Chemo. Radiation. The insurance covers some of it, but not enough. Never enough. We're drowning in medical debt. I took out a second mortgage on my house. Maxed out every credit card I have. Started a GoFundMe that raised $3,000. It's still not enough."

She looked at me. Her eyes were empty. Like she'd cried herself dry weeks ago.

"My mother is dying. And she's going to die broke. And I can't help her because I'm broke too. Because I came forward and told the truth about Tyler Carrington, and it cost me everything."

Her voice cracked.

"I can't ask my mother to die in debt while I spend years fighting him in court. I can't do that to her. I won't."

Jessica was the last to speak. She didn't cry. Just sat there with this look on her face like she was doing math. Calculating. Figuring out if survival was worth the cost.

"I lost my job," she said finally. "The day Elena published my story, they called me into HR. 'Budget cuts,' they said. Very professional. Very apologetic. But I know why."

She laughed. It sounded like breaking glass.

"I've sent out over two hundred applications since then. Two hundred. I've gotten three interviews. No offers. No-body wants to hire the girl who accused Tyler Carrington. They don't say that, obviously. They say 'we went with an-other candidate' or 'we're moving in a different direction.' But I know."

She pushed her folder away, as if she couldn't stand to look at it anymore.

"I have an eviction notice on my door. I'm about to lose my apartment. And you know what the really funny thing is? I've been homeless before. I know exactly what it's like. The shelters. The fear. The way people look through you like you don't exist."

She looked at me. "I can't go back there. I won't survive it a second time. I barely survived it the first time."

Then she turned to face me fully.

"You have a daughter to protect. I understand that. I respect that. But what do I have? What am I supposed to sacrifice for? Justice?" She shook her head. "Justice doesn't pay rent, Olivia. It doesn't pay medical bills. It doesn't save anyone."

The weight of it pressed down on my chest like concrete.

These weren't cowards. These weren't sellouts. These were three women who'd already given everything just by coming forward. Who'd been brave when it counted. Who'd told the truth and watched it destroy their lives.

And now Margaret was making them choose between justice and survival. Between punishing Tyler and saving themselves.

It was the perfect trap.

"This is what she does," I said quietly. "This is how people like Margaret win. She waits until you're desperate. Until the cost of fighting is higher than you can possibly pay. Then she offers just enough to make surrender look like salvation."

"I know," Amanda whispered. "I know that's what this is. But I'm going to take it anyway. Because I have to."

Sarah nodded, still crying.

"I want him to pay. I want him in prison. I want the world to know what he did. But wanting doesn't change reality. And the reality is my mother is dying, and this money could give her some peace at the end."

Jessica was quiet for a moment. "Then, what are you going to do, Olivia?"

They were all looking at me now. Amanda with her red, swollen eyes. Sarah with tears still streaming down her face. Jessica with that calculating expression that was really just exhaustion wearing a mask.

Patricia was looking at me too, waiting. I thought about Grace.

This morning, playing with her toes on her mat. Giggling at absolutely nothing. Perfect and innocent and completely unaware that her mother was sitting in this conference room deciding her entire future.

Tyler had raped me. Had drugged me and tied me down and taken away my choice and my voice and nine months of my life. Had made this child I loved more than anything. And now he was offering to disappear forever in exchange for his freedom.

Margaret was offering $2 million in exchange for hundreds of millions. Safety in exchange for silence. Grace's protection in exchange for Tyler's freedom.

"I don't know... I need to think," I said.

Patricia nodded and stood up.

"We have until Monday. Three days. But Olivia—" She waited until I looked at her. "Whatever you decide, make sure it's something you can live with. Because you're going to have to live with it for a very long time."

They came back in. Margaret and her lawyers. Perfect posture. Perfect suits. Already knowing they'd won.

"We need more time," Patricia told them.

"Of course." Margaret's voice was gracious, understanding, like she was doing us a favor. "This is an important decision. Take the weekend. We'll need your answers by Monday."

Sterling started packing up his folders.

Margaret stood, smoothed her suit, and looked at each of us like we were items on a spreadsheet. Problems solved. Liabilities managed.

"I understand this is difficult," she said. "But sometimes the right choice isn't the satisfying one. It's simply the choice that lets you move forward with your life."

She picked up her purse, designer, probably costing more than my car.

"Two million dollars. Freedom from litigation. Privacy. Peace. Or years of legal battles with no guaranteed outcome. Your names in the news. Your trauma relived in depositions and cross-examinations. Your lives on hold while lawyers argue."

She looked directly at me now.

"And for you specifically, Ms. Parker. Your daughter's safety. Her future. A clean break from my family. That's worth more than any amount of money."

She paused at the door.

"Choose wisely. For your daughter's sake."

Then, she was gone.

And I was left sitting in that conference room with the knowledge that Margaret was right. Grace's safety was worth more than anything. Even if it meant trading billions for millions. Even if it meant Margaret won and Tyler walked free.

Linda was in the kitchen making dinner. Grace was in her high chair.

She looked up, saw me, and her whole face lit up. She kicked her legs and waved her arms, making this sound. Half squeal, half laugh that meant *Mama!* even though she couldn't say the word yet.

I picked her up. Sweet potato in her hair, on her face, on her clothes. She grabbed my face with both sticky hands and pressed her forehead against mine. This new thing she'd started doing. Her way of saying she'd missed me.

"I missed you too, baby."

She made "Mamamama" sounds that weren't quite words yet but were trying to be. Then she wrapped her arms around my neck and squeezed as tight as her nine-month-old strength could manage.

Linda looked at me. She saw something in my face.

"What happened?"

I put Grace back in her high chair, gave her a cracker, and watched her attack it with intense concentration. Then I told Linda everything.

The offer. The money. The other women. The unanimous requirement. Tyler giving up custody. The estate waiver.

All of it.

Linda listened. She didn't interrupt. She just listened. When I finished, she was quiet for a long time.

"What do you want to do?" she finally asked.

"I want Tyler in prison. I want him to face what he did. I want the world to know he's a rapist who got away with it because his mommy has billions of dollars."

"But?"

"But Grace needs me. And Amanda needs that money. And Sarah's mother is dying. And Jessica's about to be homeless."

I looked at my daughter, covered in sweet potato. Perfectly innocent. Perfectly unaware that her mother was about to make a choice that would haunt her for the rest of her life.

"And if I say no, I'm not just fighting for justice. I'm destroying three women's lives. I'm gambling with Grace's safety for the chance... just the chance that maybe Tyler gets convicted."

"And if the jury finds him not guilty?"

"Then he walks free anyway. And I have nothing. No money. No protection. No guarantee he won't come after Grace again."

Linda reached across the table and took my hand.

"Then you already know your answer."

"I hate it."

"I know."

"It feels like giving up. Like letting them win."

"It is letting them win." Linda squeezed my hand. "But sometimes winning and surviving aren't the same thing. And you have to survive. For her."

She nodded at Grace. My daughter. The reason for everything. I couldn't protect justice. But I could protect her.

That night I couldn't sleep. I lay there watching the ceiling, listening to Grace breathe through the monitor, and watching the clock.

2 AM. 3 AM. 4 AM.

My brain wouldn't stop. It just kept replaying everything. Margaret's face, Sterling's careful words, the number on that contract.

Two million dollars for hundreds of millions. Around 4:30, I heard footsteps in the hallway. A soft knock.

"You awake?" Linda's voice came through the door.

"Yeah."

She came in and sat on the edge of my bed like she used to when we were kids and I had nightmares. For a while, we just sat in the dark, listening to Grace's soft breathing through the monitor.

"I keep thinking about the inheritance," I said finally. "Grace is Tyler's biological daughter. She could be entitled to hundreds of millions someday. And I'm about to sign it all away for two million and a promise."

Linda was quiet, processing.

"Do you really think Grace wants to be a Carrington?" she asked.

"That's not the point."

"Isn't it? You think she wants Tyler's money? Margaret's empire?"

Linda shifted to look at me. "You think she wants to be tied to that family forever? To have to explain who her father is? What he did? To fight them for every penny while they drag her through court for years?"

I hadn't thought about it like that.

"She's nine months old," Linda continued. "She can't make this choice. So you're making it for her. And you're choosing safety over money. That's not wrong, Olivia. That's love."

"Margaret's paying eight million total to protect billions. It's the deal of the century. For her."

"Maybe." Linda pulled her knees up and got comfortable. "Or maybe you're getting the better deal. Grace grows up free. No Carrington name. No Carrington expectations. No inheritance battles when Tyler or Margaret die. Just a clean break and enough money to build a good life."

She paused.

"Two million dollars and freedom from that family? That's not nothing."

"It feels like I'm selling her out."

"You're buying her freedom. There's a difference."

I wanted to believe that. I wanted it so badly.

"When I was growing up," Linda said quietly, "I used to think about what it would cost to make your grandfather go away. Not die. Just... disappear. Leave us alone forever."

She was quiet for a moment.

"I would've given anything for that. Any amount of money. Any promise. Any deal with any devil. Just to make him stop."

Grace made a sound through the monitor. A soft sleep-whimper. Then quiet again.

"That's what Margaret's really offering you," Linda continued. "Not money. Safety. Tyler disappears forever. Grace never has to know him. Never has to face him. You're not selling her out. You're buying her freedom from him."

"You really think so?"

"I know so. Because I wish your grandmother had chosen me and your aunt over your grandfather. Just once. But she never did." Linda squeezed my hand. "You're different. You're choosing your daughter over everything else. That's what matters."

We sat there a while longer in the dark room, listening to the soft monitor sounds.

"I wish we lived in a world where doing the right thing didn't cost everything," Linda said finally. "Where justice was something you could actually afford."

"Yeah."

"But we don't. We live in this one, where Margaret Carrington has billions and you have a baby who needs her mother." She stood up. "So you take the money, keep Grace safe, and move on with your life."

After she left, I picked up my phone and stared at it for a long time in the dark. Then I called Amanda.

She answered on the second ring, like she hadn't been sleeping either.

"Olivia?"

"I'm taking the settlement."

She started crying immediately. Big, shaking sobs.

"Thank you," she whispered. "Thank you. I'm so sorry. I'm so sorry."

"Don't be sorry. You didn't do anything wrong."

"I feel like I'm betraying you. Like I'm letting him win."

"You're not betraying me. You're surviving. That's all any of us can do."

After we hung up, I texted Sarah: *I'm in. Take care of your mom.*

She replied immediately: *I don't know how to thank you.*

You don't have to. Just be okay.

Jessica called instead of texting.

"You're sure?" she asked.

"No. But I'm doing it anyway."

"For Grace?"

"For Grace. And for you guys. I can't take that money away from you. I won't."

"We could fight together. All four of us. Maybe—"

"Jessica. You're about to lose your apartment. Sarah's mom is dying. Amanda's drowning in debt. There's no 'maybe' that's worth what it would cost you to keep fighting."

She was quiet. Then: "I wanted him to pay."

"Me too."

"But wanting doesn't change anything, does it?"

"No. It doesn't."

Monday morning, we met back at Sterling & Katz.

Same conference room. Same marble and glass and views that made Chicago look small and manageable and owned.

Same four women. But different now. Changed.

Patricia had reviewed every page of the contracts with a team of lawyers. She made sure there were no hidden traps, no secret clauses that would come back to destroy us later.

The terms were clear:

$2,000,000 per plaintiff.

Non-disclosure agreements prohibiting any discussion of Tyler Carrington or the allegations. Release of all civil claims.

For me specifically: a separate agreement where Tyler permanently withdrew from all custody proceedings and relinquished all parental rights to Grace.

And the estate waiver. The provision that made Grace a stranger to the Carrington fortune. Two million dollars now in exchange for hundreds of millions she'd never see.

Margaret wasn't there this time. She didn't need to be. She'd already won.

Just Sterling and two other lawyers. Professional. Polite. Ready to collect our signatures and make this go away.

"Any questions before we proceed?" Sterling asked.

"Just one," I said. "Once we sign this and stop cooperating with the DA, Tyler faces no criminal charges. Is that correct?"

"The Cook County District Attorney will make their own determination about whether to proceed. But without victim cooperation, they will lack the evidence necessary to build a case." Sterling's voice was careful. "So yes, in practical terms, Mr. Carrington will face no criminal prosecution."

"He gets away with raping four women."

"The allegations will be resolved through this civil settlement."

"That's not an answer."

Sterling looked at me. His expression never changed.

"It's the only answer you're going to get, Ms. Parker."

I looked down at the contract in front of me. I found the page with the estate waiver. I read it one more time.

The undersigned hereby irrevocably waives any and all claims, for herself and on behalf of the minor child Grace Parker, to inheritance, trust funds, estate distributions, or any other financial consideration from Tyler James Carrington, Margaret Elizabeth Carrington, Carrington Media Group, or any associated entities or trusts, whether arising from bio-

logical relationship, legal relationship, or any other connection, in perpetuity.

In perpetuity. Forever.

I picked up the pen and signed my name on the first page. Then the second. Then the third. Olivia Parker. Over and over. My signature selling my silence.

Beside me, Amanda signed. Her hands were shaking, but she got through it.

Sarah went next. Tears streamed down her face as she signed each page.

Jessica signed last. No emotion. Just got it done. Like ripping off a bandage all at once.

Sterling collected the contracts. He examined each signature and nodded to one of the other lawyers.

The lawyer pulled out four cashier's checks from a folder and slid them across the table.

$2,000,000.00

More money than I'd ever seen in my life. More money than I'd ever imagined having. The price of my silence. The price of my daughter's safety. The price of letting a rapist walk free.

I picked up the check. The paper felt heavier than it should have.

"The custody withdrawal will be filed with the court this afternoon," Sterling said. "By the end of business today, you will have sole legal and physical custody of your daughter. Mr. Carrington will have no rights. No contact. No claims."

"And if he violates that?"

"He won't. This agreement is legally binding. Any violation would expose him to significant liability."

I put the check in my purse, stood up, and walked out of that conference room without looking back.

In the elevator, Amanda hugged me.

"We did the right thing," she said. "We did."

But her voice cracked on the words, like she was trying to convince herself.

Sarah hugged me next. She whispered, "Thank you," into my shoulder.

Jessica didn't hug. She just squeezed my hand once. Hard.

"It's not over," she said quietly. "This isn't how the story ends."

"Then how does it end?"

"I don't know. But not like this. Not with him walking away clean."

The elevator doors opened onto the lobby, and all hell broke loose.

Reporters everywhere. Cameras. Microphones. Lights.

Someone had tipped them off. Probably Margaret's people. Controlling the narrative. Making sure the story got out the way she wanted.

Questions shouted from every direction:

"Ms. Parker! Did you settle with Tyler Carrington?"

"Is it true he paid you two million dollars?"

"Do you still stand by your allegations?"

"Was this about money all along?"

I couldn't answer. The NDA was already in effect. One word and I'd be in breach of contract.

Patricia materialized beside me and started steering me toward the exit.

"No comment. My clients have no comment."

"Ms. Lopez! Why did you take the settlement?"

Amanda's face crumpled. She turned away.

"Ms. Mitchell! Are you dropping the charges?"

Sarah kept her head down and walked faster.

"Ms. Ramirez! Do you regret coming forward?"

Jessica stopped and turned to face the cameras. For a second, I thought she was going to break. Going to tell them everything. Violate the NDA and blow up the whole settlement.

But she just looked into the cameras and said, "We did what we had to do to survive. That's all." Then she turned and walked away.

Outside, the cold air hit my face like a slap. Patricia's car was at the curb. She pushed me toward it.

"Get in. Don't look back. Don't say anything."

I got in. Through the window, I could see the reporters still shouting. Still trying to get a comment. A reaction. Something they could turn into a headline.

"Carrington Accusers Take Settlement: Was It About Justice or Money?"

I could already see it.

Patricia pulled away from the curb. The reporters got smaller in the rearview mirror.

"You okay?" she asked.

"No."

"Yeah. I figured."

She drove me home in silence. What was there to say?

Linda was waiting with Grace when I got home.

My daughter was on her playmat. She had recently discovered her feet and was fascinated by them. She grabbed them, examined them, and put them in her mouth like they might taste good.

Grace looked up when I walked in. She smiled her gummy smile and reached for me. I picked her up, held her close, and breathed in the smell of her hair. Baby shampoo and milk and something uniquely Grace.

Tyler would never touch her. Never see her. Never have any claim to her. She was mine. Only mine. Safe. And it only cost everything I believed in.

Linda came over and put her hand on my back.

"You did it."

"Yeah."

"Grace is safe."

"Yeah."

"Then it was worth it."

Was it?

I didn't know. I might never know. But my daughter was in my arms. Warm and solid and real. And that had to be enough.

The news broke that afternoon.

It started on social media, then picked up by real outlets, then everywhere.

"Breaking: Four Women Settle Civil Claims Against Tyler Carrington"

"Carrington Rape Case Dropped After Settlement"

"Justice or Payday? Tyler Carrington Accusers Take Multi-Million Dollar Settlement"

The comments section was exactly what I expected:

I knew she was lying.

Gold diggers, all of them.

They got their payday; that's all they wanted.

If he really raped them, why would they settle?

But there were other comments too. Quieter. Fewer. But there:

The system failed them.

What choice did they have?

She's a mother protecting her daughter.

Rich men always buy their way out.

I read the comments for about five minutes, then put my phone in a drawer and didn't look at it for the rest of the day.

What strangers thought didn't matter. Tyler had won. Margaret had won. And I'd chosen to let them win.

That was the truth. Everything else was just noise.

Detective Smith called the next day.

"Olivia."

His voice was tired. Defeated.

"The DA officially closed the case this morning. Without victim cooperation, they don't have enough to proceed." Long pause. "I'm sorry."

"Don't be. I made my choice."

"For what it's worth... I get it. I've got kids too."

"Yeah."

"But your daughter is safe. That counts for something."

"Does it?"

"It has to."

After he hung up, I sat in Grace's room and watched her sleep.

Grace rolled over in her crib and made that little sound she makes when she's dreaming. Soft and content.

She'd never know the fear I'd carried these past months. The terror of losing her to the man who raped me. She'd grow up safe. Loved. Protected. By a mother who'd made an impossible choice.

A week later, Patricia filed the official paperwork: Tyler's withdrawal from custody proceedings. My sole legal and physical custody of Grace.

No visitation. No contact. No claims. Forever.

The judge signed it without a hearing. No drama. No fight. Just signatures and stamps and legal language that meant my daughter was mine.

I should have felt relief. Victory. Something. Instead, I just felt empty. Like I'd won a war by surrendering.

Tomorrow, I'd deposit the check. Two million dollars. Tyler's blood money. The price of my silence.

I opened my nightstand drawer. The cedar box was there. I'd brought it from Linda's shed after that night I'd almost drunk. A reminder of what I'd chosen.

The compass sat on faded velvet. Cracked glass. The needle spun weakly.

Dad had given it to me when I was eight. *"You're my compass, Olivia. You always know what's right."*

But what was right now?

The needle spun. North. South. East. West. It couldn't settle on any direction.

Maybe that was the truth Dad never told me. The compass doesn't tell you which way is right. It just shows you there is a north. You still have to choose which direction that is. And some choices don't have a right answer. Just consequences you have to live with.

I closed the box. Put it back in the drawer.

But tonight, I just lay there listening to my daughter breathe. Wondering if she'd ever understand why I'd made this choice. Wondering if I'd ever forgive myself for making it.

The compass was in the drawer. Still broken. Still spinning. And I was here. Still sober. Still showing up.

That had to count for something, even if I couldn't see what yet.

Chapter Eight

The Obsession Begins

Grace was ten months old. The check was in my purse. I stood at the bank counter holding two million dollars.

The teller took one look at the amount, and her eyes went wide. She excused herself and disappeared into the back.

I stood there, people in line behind me, shifting, impatient, checking their phones.

A man in an expensive suit came out. Perfect hair. Perfect smile. He extended his hand.

"Ms. Parker? I'm Richard, the branch manager. Would you be more comfortable discussing your needs in my office?"

The way he said "needs" made it clear this wasn't a suggestion.

I followed him past the regular bank area into a hallway with actual carpet. His office had wood paneling, leather chairs, and framed awards on the walls.

"Please, sit." He gestured to a chair that probably cost more than my rent. "Can I offer you coffee? We have an espresso machine."

Real coffee. Not break room drip.

"Water's fine."

He brought me water in an actual glass, not a paper cup. Glass.

Then he sat across from me with a warm, attentive expression I'd never seen on a banker's face before.

"How can we assist you today?"

Assist me. Like I was someone who mattered.

I handed him the check. He glanced at it and didn't even blink, as if two million dollars was normal. Expected.

"Wonderful. And what type of account would you like to establish?"

"What do you recommend?"

He pulled out a leather folder. "I should mention our private banking services. For clients of your caliber, we offer wealth management, investment advisory, tax planning, and trust services—"

"What about an S&P 500 index fund?" I interrupted him.

Richard paused and looked at me differently, as if I'd said something significant.

"That's an excellent choice. Low cost, diversified, simple."

I'd learned about it at McKinsey. The S&P 500. Five hundred of the largest companies in America: Google, Apple, Microsoft, Amazon. The safest bet you could make in the stock market without picking individual stocks.

"Historical returns average around ten percent annually. That's roughly two hundred thousand a year on two million dollars," Richard said as he pulled out different paperwork.

"We can set up a brokerage account and invest the full amount in a low-cost S&P 500 index fund, Vanguard or Fidelity. Your choice."

The math hit me. Two hundred thousand dollars a year. Just from the money sitting there. Growing. Compounding.

Blood money earning more blood money. But at least it would be doing something. Not just rotting in savings. Not just sitting there reminding me what I'd sold.

"Let's do that," I heard myself say.

Richard processed everything. He handed me a leather portfolio with my account information. His business card was embossed on heavy paper that felt luxurious.

"Please call anytime, Ms. Parker. Day or night. The bank values your relationship."

He walked me out personally, shook my hand again, and thanked me for choosing their bank.

I walked to my car holding the leather portfolio.

I'd never been treated like this. At McKinsey, I'd been entry-level. Invisible. At the diner, I'd been the help. Growing up, I'd been overlooked.

Now, because of a number on a check, I was suddenly worth white-glove service. The money was buying me respect. Deference. Attention. And it made everything worse because I knew what I'd paid for it.

Grace cried from the other room. I tried to put her to sleep.

It was 7 PM. Grace was exhausted. I could see it in her face, the way her eyes drooped, the way she kept rubbing her fists against her cheeks.

But sleep wouldn't come easy. It never did.

I took her upstairs to Linda's guest room. Grace's crib was in the corner, along with her blankets and her stuffed animals that she couldn't really play with yet.

I changed her diaper. She cried through it. Everything was too much at the end of the day. Too tired to regulate. Too overwhelmed to cope.

I got her into pajamas, the soft ones, the only ones she tolerated. I'd bought three identical pairs so I'd always have a clean set.

I picked her up and started rocking. She was stiff in my arms, not melting, not settling. I tried singing the lullaby Linda used to sing to me and Leo when we were little.

Grace cried harder. I tried the white noise machine, the one that cost $80 because it had to be the right frequency. Not too high, not too low.

She screamed. I walked her around the room, bouncing gently, shushing, trying everything.

Nothing worked. An hour passed. Grace was hysterical now, overtired and unable to calm down. Her nervous system was stuck in fight-or-flight with no way to reset.

I was crying too. Exhausted. Overwhelmed. Two million dollars in the bank, and I couldn't get my daughter to sleep.

Linda knocked on the door. "Need help?"

"I don't know what she needs."

Linda came in, dimmed the lights even more, and closed the curtains tighter.

"Let me try."

She took Grace and wrapped her tightly in the weighted blanket. Pressure. Deep pressure that helped Grace's nervous system calm.

Grace fought it at first. Then slowly, slowly, she started to settle.

Linda sat in the rocking chair, held Grace close against her chest, and rocked in a steady rhythm. Not fast. Not slow. Just steady.

After twenty minutes, Grace's crying stopped. After thirty, her eyes started to close. After forty-five, she was asleep.

Linda stood slowly, carried her to the crib, and laid her down on her back. Grace stirred but didn't wake.

We both stood there watching her breathe, making sure she stayed down.

"It takes her so long to settle," I whispered. "Other babies just... go to sleep."

"Other babies don't have FASD."

The words hung there. True. Terrible. Permanent.

"The money will help," Linda said quietly. "You can afford the best therapists now, the best specialists, and the special needs preschool when she's older."

I looked at Grace, her chest rising and falling, the scar from her heart surgery barely visible in the dim light.

"Two million dollars came from selling my silence about rape, and I'm going to use it to pay for fixing the damage from vodka."

"You're going to use it to give her the best life possible," Linda corrected. "That's not the same thing."

We were quiet for a moment. Grace slept. The white noise machine hummed. The weighted blanket rose and fell with her breathing.

I watched my daughter sleep. Ten months old. Should be babbling, playing, exploring. Instead, she needed weighted blankets, white noise machines, and 90 minutes to calm down enough to sleep.

Linda touched my shoulder. "Come on. Let her sleep. You need sleep too."

We left the door cracked, the white noise machine humming, and the night light glowing soft blue.

A couple of months went by. Grace was twelve months old, but different. Stronger. Late one night, I couldn't sleep.

I sat in the rocking chair in her room, watching her breathe. Her chest rising and falling. Easy. Steady. Her repaired heart doing its job.

I looked at Grace's face in the dark. This child who'd refused to give up. Who'd fought through death and come back.

"I'm sorry, baby girl," I whispered. "I'm sorry I wasn't stronger before you."

She slept on. Peaceful. Trusting.

The air shifted. Went cold. I knew that feeling. My breath caught.

"Leo?"

He was standing in the corner. Same as always. Sixteen years old forever, wearing the hoodie he'd died in.

I hadn't seen him since that night in the shed. When I'd been pregnant and ready to drink Dad's vodka. When he'd appeared in the shadows and stopped me.

I thought that was the last time.

"You're really here," I whispered.

He moved closer. His face was sad but peaceful. The same look he'd had when we were kids and he'd find me hiding in the closet from Dad.

"I'm here, Livvy."

He looked at Grace sleeping in her crib. "She's beautiful."

"She's everything."

"I know." He turned back to me. "That's why I came."

My chest tightened. "Why?"

"Because you keep torturing yourself, wondering if you made the right choice."

The settlement. He meant the settlement.

"I let him walk free, Leo. I took his money and let him walk away."

"You saved her." He nodded at Grace. "You chose her safety over revenge. That's what love looks like."

"But he hurt me. Hurt three other women. And now he's free, running a company, living his life like nothing happened."

"Yeah." Leo's voice was gentle. "And you're here. Sober. Taking care of your daughter. Breaking every cycle we grew up with."

"It doesn't feel like enough."

"It's everything."

I started crying. I couldn't help it.

"I miss you so much."

"I know. But Livvy—" He waited until I looked at him. "You did the right thing. Taking that money. Protecting Grace. Staying sober through all of it. I'm so proud of you."

"You shouldn't be. I'm a coward."

"You're a survivor." His voice was firm, the way it used to get when he'd defend me to Dad. "You're a mother. You're sober. You're fighting. That's not cowardice. That's courage."

"Then why does it hurt so much?"

"Because you're alive to feel it." He looked at Grace again. "She's alive because of you. Because you stayed sober. Because you made impossible choices. Because you keep showing up."

I wiped my eyes and looked at my daughter, her tiny chest rising and falling.

"I wanted you to save me," Leo said quietly. "When I was dying on that concrete. I wanted you to answer your phone, come running, fix it."

The guilt slammed into me.

"I should have—"

"No." He cut me off. "You were asleep. Studying. Living your life. You couldn't have known."

"But if I had just—"

"Livvy." He moved closer. "You can't save everyone. You couldn't save me. You can't get justice for what Tyler did. But you can save yourself. You can raise Grace. You can stay sober. You can choose to keep fighting."

"Is that enough?"

"It has to be."

We sat in silence. Grace made a small sound in her sleep and settled.

"I should let you go," Leo said. "You don't need to see me anymore. You're doing well without the ghosts."

"I love you," I whispered.

"I love you too." He started fading. "Take care of my niece. Stay sober. Keep fighting. You're doing better than you know."

Then, he was gone.

The room was warm again. Normal temperature.

I sat there shaking, crying silently so I wouldn't wake Grace. Leo had said I'd made the right choice. He'd said I was doing well. He'd said to keep fighting.

I looked at my daughter. Her perfect face, her steady breathing.

"I promise you," I whispered. "I promise on everything I am. I'll never drink again. Not one drop. Not ever. You're my reason. You showed me how to be strong."

It was the same promise I'd made before, when she was born, when she survived surgery. But it felt different now. Deeper.

About staying sober, yes. But more than that. About being worthy of this child who never quit. About matching her strength with my own.

I sat in that chair until dawn, watching her breathe, watching her live. She'd fought her way back from death. I could fight my way back from everything else.

And Leo thought I was doing okay. That had to count for something.

After things settled down, I was finally getting back to my normal life. I was at a coffee shop, one of the nice ones I could afford now. Grace was in her stroller, eating banana pieces, getting healthier with each passing day.

I ordered a latte without looking at the price. Still getting used to having money. It still felt wrong somehow.

I sat down and opened my phone to check the news.

And everything stopped.

Carrington Media Names Tyler Carrington CEO: Next Generation Takes the Helm

There was a photo. Tyler in an expensive suit, standing in a boardroom with Margaret beside him, both smiling.

I read the article. Couldn't stop reading.

"Legacy." "Family dynasty." "Innovative leadership."

Margaret referred to Tyler as "the future of Carrington Media."

Tyler discussed his "vision" for the company.

The man who had raped four women. The man who had just escaped criminal charges because his mother paid eight million dollars. The man whose DNA produced the daughter eating bananas in front of me.

He was the CEO of a multibillion-dollar media empire.

I read it three times. My coffee grew cold. Grace finished her banana and started fussing. I didn't notice.

The article detailed his background: Northwestern, previous roles at smaller media companies, his "fresh perspective," and "strategic vision."

It listed Carrington Media's holdings: local news stations across six states, radio networks, digital media, and content production.

Current stock valuation: approximately $10.1 billion.

Margaret was handing him an empire. The world would see Tyler Carrington, CEO, young media executive, legacy heir. Only four women knew the truth.

Grace began crying. She was bored and wanted out. I picked her up automatically, still staring at my phone. I screenshotted the article, saved it, and didn't know why.

Then I searched "Tyler Carrington CEO" and found more: business journals, trade publications, everyone covering the appointment.

I read them all while walking Grace around the coffee shop, bouncing her on my hip, not really seeing where I was going.

That night, after Grace was asleep, I opened my laptop and searched "Carrington Media Group."

I found their corporate website, annual reports, and press releases. I started reading.

I told myself it was just curiosity, just wanting to understand what kind of company he was running. But something else was happening. Something colder.

I created a folder on my desktop labeled "CMG." I saved the annual report, the press releases, and articles about the CEO transition.

I stared at the folder for a long time. Tyler had taken everything from me. Now he was being given everything. I wanted to know every detail of what he had. I needed to see it all.

I couldn't stop reading about Carrington Media. It started innocently enough. Checking the news, following business coverage, keeping informed.

But it wasn't innocent. I was obsessed.

I read every press release the day it was released. I signed up for investor relations emails, downloaded quarterly reports, and read trade publications that covered the media industry.

I set up Google alerts: "Tyler Carrington" and "Carrington Media."

My phone buzzed constantly.

Grace napped, and I opened my laptop. Grace played, and I scrolled through media trade news. Grace went to bed, and I dove into financial filings.

I told myself I was keeping my skills sharp, staying informed, using my brain. The truth was darker: I was stalking him through business news, stock prices, and earnings reports.

And I couldn't stop. Another month passed. I started really studying. Beyond just reading the news, I was diving deep.

Media companies: how they operated, how they made money, how they were structured. I didn't know why. I didn't know what I was trying to learn or what I'd do with the information. But I needed to understand.

I'd always been good at this, even as a kid. When things got bad at home, I'd disappear into books, into learning, into studying things that took me away from reality.

School had been my escape, not because I loved it, but because I was good at it. And being skilled at something gave me control when everything else was chaos.

I did the same thing now. I downloaded textbooks about media economics, read case studies about successful media companies, and studied industry reports on market trends.

I learned about advertising revenue models, subscription economics, content licensing, distribution channels, and digital transformation strategies. I was teaching myself how media companies operated from the ground up.

Grace was on the floor with her toys scattered around her, reaching for blocks and knocking them over, laughing at the noise they made.

I was at the kitchen table with my laptop, reading about broadcast television economics. Linda came over and saw me surrounded by papers and notes.

"What are you doing?"

"Research."

"For what?"

I didn't have an answer.

"Just learning," I finally said.

Linda looked skeptical but didn't push.

Before I knew it, my CMG folder became huge, with sub-folders for everything: financials, acquisitions, executive team, board members, market analysis, and competitive landscape.

I knew Carrington Media's business better than most of their employees probably did.

Revenue breakdown by segment, profit margins by division, debt structure, capital allocation strategy, growth initiatives.

I'd created spreadsheets, tracked everything, charted trends, and built models.

It was what I'd done at McKinsey: take a company, understand it completely, find the patterns, identify the risks. Except at McKinsey, I'd been paid to do it.

Now I was doing it alone, in the dark, consumed by an inexplicable obsession.

Grace toddled over. "Mama, play?"

I closed the laptop and sat down on the floor with her. We played with dolls. I was present. I was there. But part of my mind was elsewhere: on Tyler, on Carrington Media, on the empire he was running, and on everything I was learning about how it all worked.

I didn't know why it mattered, but I couldn't stop.

Chapter Nine

Finding the Crack

TYLER'S FIRST PRESS CONFERENCE as CEO resembled a coronation.

Grace was eighteen months old. I was trying to get her to eat breakfast, but she kept dropping the spoon. Her fingers wouldn't grip right. Motor delays that would probably never fully catch up.

I gave up after twenty minutes and fed her myself while watching my laptop on the counter.

Tyler was in a perfect suit, and Margaret stood beside him, beaming. Reporters gathered as if he were royalty.

He talked about "transformational leadership" and a "bold vision for the future." He used words like "disruption" and "innovation" the way others used punctuation.

The banner on CNBC read: **NEW ERA FOR CAR-RINGTON MEDIA.**

Jim Cramer on Mad Money called him "a fresh voice in legacy media."

Margaret's face glowed with pride. "Tyler represents everything this company can become. He's fearless. He's brilliant. He's ready."

I wiped oatmeal from Grace's face, cleaned her hands, and lifted her from the high chair.

Tyler was being handed ten billion dollars and a company that had survived three recessions. I wondered how long it would take him to destroy it.

Three months later, I found out.

CARRINGTON MEDIA ACQUIRES STREAM-MEDIA FOR $800 MILLION.

The alert came through while I was at the playground. I stopped mid-push on Grace's swing to read it.

"Higher, Mama!"

"Just a second, baby."

I pulled up StreamMedia's financials on my phone. My fingers trembled before I finished reading the first page.

Subscribers were down thirty-five percent. They were burning sixty million a quarter, competing against Netflix and Disney in a war they'd already lost.

Even rusty, I could see this was wrong. Tyler had just paid eight hundred million dollars for a company worth maybe less than half of that.

That night, after Grace finally fell asleep, I did something I hadn't done in four years.

I opened my laptop and pulled up my old McKinsey files. The frameworks. The analytical templates, the valuation models I'd built and thought I'd never touch again.

My hands were shaking. Not from fear, but from something else.

Recognition, maybe. I knew this feeling, this pull, this need to understand everything.

I'd felt it at sixteen. Studying until 3 AM because understanding calculus meant escape from Millfield. Because perfect grades meant McKinsey, which meant freedom from Dad's rage.

I'd felt it at Ohio State. Every case study memorized. Every framework mastered. Obsessed with learning because knowledge was the only thing I could control.

Now I felt it again. But this time it wasn't about escape. It was about understanding my enemy.

In addition to general knowledge, I had to relearn specialized finance concepts. I enrolled in three online courses that week.

Financial Statement Analysis. Corporate Valuation. Mergers and Acquisitions. Cost: $237 total. I needed this more than I needed anything else.

Linda saw the charges on our shared credit card and came into my room that evening while I was taking notes on balance sheet analysis.

"You're taking finance classes?"

"Relearning what I used to know."

"Why?"

I didn't have an answer that would make sense to her. How could I explain that I needed to see through Tyler's every move? That I needed to understand every decision he made, every acquisition, every deal, every lie hidden in quarterly earnings reports?

"I just need to get my skills back."

Linda sat on the edge of my bed and looked at my laptop screen. Pages of notes. Financial ratios. Valuation formulas.

"This is about Tyler."

"It's about remembering what I'm capable of."

"Olivia." Her voice was gentle but firm. "You need to let this go. He's living his life. You need to live yours."

"I am living my life."

"Are you? Or are you spending every night obsessed with the company run by the man who hurt you?"

Grace made a sound from her crib. A small whimper. Not quite awake.

"It's just a few classes," I said quietly.

But we both knew it was more than that.

I studied the way I used to study before McKinsey. Before everything fell apart.

Every night after Grace went to sleep. Every naptime. Every quiet moment. I watched lecture videos at 1.5x speed. Took notes in the same careful handwriting I'd used in college. Worked practice problems until my hand cramped.

Module 1: Reading Balance Sheets. Module 2: Income Statement Analysis. Module 3: Cash Flow Statements.

The terminology flooded back. Assets. Liabilities. Free cash flow. Return on invested capital. I'd memorized these definitions as a college sophomore. Had used them every day at McKinsey. Had been good at this once.

Now I was relearning concepts I used to know without thinking. It was humbling, but also familiar, like finding a part of myself I'd buried.

By week three, I'd finished all three courses, downloaded the certificates, and opened a new folder on my laptop.

CMG Analysis

Carrington Media Group. Tyler's company. My enemy.

I pulled Carrington's last three years of financial statements. Public companies had to file them; anyone could see them.

I started building a model: revenue by segment, cost structure, debt levels, and capital allocation.

It took me four days, working every spare minute. Grace played at my feet while I typed, and Linda shot me worried looks when she came home from work.

But I couldn't stop. I didn't want to stop.

This felt like the old Olivia. The girl who'd studied her way out of Millfield and who'd gotten into McKinsey through pure obsession and determination. Except now I wasn't studying to escape; I was studying to understand, to see every weakness in Tyler's empire, every bad decision, every vulnerability.

Because someday I might need to know. Someday I might be able to use it. And I wanted to be ready.

Grace woke me up at 6 AM. Not crying. Making sounds. She was sitting up in her crib by herself, with no support. My chest tightened.

Grace was two years old. Most kids her age had been sitting up for over a year. Some were already potty training, having conversations, and running. Grace had only mastered sitting a few months ago, and now she was doing something else: trying to stand.

Her little hands gripped the crib rail, white-knuckled. Her legs shook with effort. She pulled, strained, and her face turned red. She fell back onto her padded diaper bottom.

She made a sound: frustration, pure determination, anger at her own body for not working the way she wanted. Then she tried again.

"Mama!"

She pulled herself up again. Stood. Five seconds this time. Her whole face lit up with pride and joy, as if she'd just conquered the world.

"I see you! You're so strong!"

"Strong!" she repeated, her favorite new word, the one her physical therapist taught her.

She let go of the rail with one hand, testing to see if she could do it. She wobbled, grabbed back on fast, and laughed again.

This child I'd damaged before she was born. This daughter conceived in violence who shouldn't even be alive. This baby who'd died on an operating table for eight seconds and fought her way back. She was fighting every single day to do things that came naturally to other kids.

And she did it with joy, with laughter, with a determination that put me to shame.

She'd been doing this every day in therapy for months. Falling. Trying. Falling. Trying. The therapists kept telling me the same thing: "She has more determination than any child we've worked with. Most kids her age get frustrated and quit. Grace never quits."

Now I understood where it came from. From something deeper. Something that had kept her alive through heart surgery and FASD and a mother who'd poisoned her. Grace was a fighter. Always had been. Since before she was born.

And watching her now, I realized something that made me feel sick. I was spending every waking hour obsessing over Tyler. But Grace was right here. Fighting her own battles. Making her own progress. Doing the impossible every single day. And I was missing it.

How many times had she tried to stand this week while I was on my laptop? How many small victories had I missed because I was reading earnings reports?

She let go with both hands. Stood unsupported for two full seconds. Her eyes went wide. Shocked at her own success. Then she fell but grabbed the rail before she hit the bottom.

"Did it!" she shouted. "Mama, did it!"

"You did it, baby! You're amazing!"

My voice broke completely. Tears streamed down my face. She laughed. Pure joy. Just the happiness of trying something hard and getting a little bit better.

She was two years old. Would never be "normal." Would struggle her entire life with things other people did without thinking. But she was happy. Fighting. Trying. While I drowned in bitterness and rage.

Linda appeared in the doorway behind me, hair messy from sleep. She saw me on the floor, crying, watching Grace.

"She's standing?" Her voice was gentle.

"Almost." I wiped my face. "She's so close."

Linda slid down the wall and sat beside me on the floor. We watched together, Grace trying over and over. Sometimes standing for three seconds. Sometimes falling immediately. Never giving up.

"She gets that from you," Linda said quietly.

"What?"

"That determination. That refusal to quit." Linda looked at me. "You used to study like that. Remember? For college. For McKinsey. Hours and hours until you mastered it."

Grace fell hard. She started to cry for real this time. Exhausted. I went to her quickly. Picked her up. She clung to me like I was the only solid thing in the world.

"Tired, Mama." Her voice was so small.

"I know, baby. You worked so hard. So, so hard."

She rested her head on my shoulder. Her breathing already slowing. She'd be asleep in minutes. The way she always did after therapy. After pushing herself past every limit.

I rocked her gently. Felt her weight. Her warmth. Her complete trust that I would keep her safe.

"She's getting better," I whispered. "Slower than other kids. But she's getting there."

"She is," Linda agreed. "Because she doesn't give up. And because you show up every day to help her."

I looked at my laptop through the doorway. The CMG folder. The spreadsheets. The obsession that was consuming me. "But I'm not showing up," I said. My voice broke. "I'm here physically. But mentally I'm with him. With Tyler. With the company. With everything I'm trying to understand so I can—"

"So you can what?" Linda pressed.

"I don't know!" The words came out too loud. Grace stirred but didn't wake.

"I don't know, okay? I just need to know. Need to see everything. Because even though he can't technically take Grace anymore by contract, I have this bad feeling that he will take her someday. I need to know every weakness, every lie."

Linda was quiet for a long time. Grace was asleep now, exhausted from her victory, thumb in her mouth, face peaceful.

"You're right," Linda said finally.

"You're human. You're traumatized. You're terrified." Linda put her hand on my shoulder. "But you can't spend her childhood obsessing over him. You just can't. Because she's going to wake up one day, and you're going to realize you missed it. You missed her learning to stand, to walk, to talk, to be herself. Because you were too busy studying the man who hurt you."

I pressed my face against Grace's hair. I let myself cry for real.

"I don't know how to stop," I admitted. "I don't know how to let it go."

"I know. But you have to try. For her."

I carried Grace back to her crib. She curled up immediately, still clutching the rail even in her sleep. Still fighting, even in her dreams. Tomorrow she'd try again. And the day after. And the day after that. Until she could stand, then walk, then run. One impossible thing at a time.

Standing there watching Grace sleep, I wondered if I was already too far gone. Too obsessed. Too consumed by rage to find my way back.

But deep down, I knew the truth. The obsession wasn't something I could just decide to stop. It was already inside me, growing, consuming. And I didn't know how to kill it before it killed everything else.

Six months into Tyler's tenure, they held their first earnings call.

I listened live. Grace was napping. I sat at the kitchen table with my laptop, taking notes like I used to at McKinsey.

Tyler started strong, delivering rehearsed remarks about "strategic positioning" and "digital transformation."

Then the analysts began asking questions.

"Tyler, can you walk us through the revenue synergies from StreamMedia? Subscriber losses seem to be accelerating."

"We're confident in the long-term trajectory." Tyler's voice was smooth and rehearsed. "Short-term metrics don't reflect the strategic value of content ownership and distribution capabilities."

I wrote that down. *Translation: no synergies. No plan.*

"But you paid six times revenue for a platform losing users at an increasing rate. Can you help us understand the math?"

A pause. Too long.

"I think you're missing the bigger picture here. This isn't about quarter-to-quarter subscriber counts. It's about positioning ourselves for—"

"The bigger picture includes an eight hundred million dollar acquisition that appears to be worth less than half that. Can you address the valuation?"

"Look." Tyler's voice sharpened. "We're not going to manage this company by looking in the rearview mirror. If you want to focus on legacy metrics instead of transformation, then maybe you don't understand where media is heading."

I sat up straighter. He was getting defensive. Angry.

Another analyst jumped in. "Tyler, your debt load has increased significantly. How are you thinking about leverage in light of the integration costs?"

"We have plenty of room on our balance sheet. Next question."

"But the debt-to-EBITDA ratio—"

"I said next question."

The silence that followed was uncomfortable. You could hear it even through the webcast.

He was deflecting. I'd been trained to spot this at McKinsey. The way executives pivoted when they didn't have answers. The defensive posture. The vague language.

When the call ended, I had three pages of notes. Red flags. Patterns. Warnings. The stock dropped eight percent that day. Then I pulled up Carrington Media's quarterly report. The actual SEC filing.

I'd done this hundreds of times at McKinsey: reading 10-Qs and 10-Ks, looking for inconsistencies, finding what companies tried to hide. The skills were rusty but coming back, like riding a bike after years away.

Joe Freyer's voice echoed in my head, my old manager at McKinsey: "Read the footnotes. That's where they bury the bodies."

It took four hours. Grace woke up from her nap. I fed her lunch while reading on my phone at the kitchen table. Applesauce in one hand, phone in the other. I put her down for quiet time and kept reading.

By dinner, I'd found something.

StreamMedia's subscriber numbers in Tyler's earnings call didn't match the numbers buried in Note 17 of the quarterly report. They were off by almost twenty percent.

I stopped breathing. Went back. Read it again, slower this time, making sure I wasn't seeing things.

The numbers were there, clear as day, buried in dense financial language on page forty-seven. But there.

Tyler had told investors StreamMedia had 8.2 million subscribers. The footnote said 6.7 million.

A chill ran down my spine, starting at the base of my skull and spreading through my whole body. I had to put my phone down on the table.

I checked twice. Three times. I pulled up StreamMedia's last public filing before the acquisition. I cross-referenced the numbers. I did the math four different ways.

Every method said the same thing: the numbers were inflated. At McKinsey, we'd had a polite name for this: "management optimism." The real name was fraud.

My heart was pounding. Actually pounding. I could feel it in my chest, in my throat, in my ears.

Tyler had lied to investors. In a public filing, in an earnings call. That was securities fraud.

I stood up fast, the chair scraping loudly against the floor. I started pacing in Linda's kitchen. My whole body felt electric, buzzing, like I'd grabbed a live wire.

Grace was in her room playing. I could hear her talking to her stuffed animals, making up stories in her limited words.

I grabbed my laptop and opened a new spreadsheet with shaking hands. I had to type the title three times because I kept hitting the wrong keys.

CMG - Irregularities

I stared at the name for a long time, my pulse racing, my mouth dry.

This was real. This was something.

I wanted to call someone. Tell someone. Linda. A lawyer. The SEC. But Joe's voice cut through the excitement: "Never show your hand until you have the full picture. One inconsistency could be a mistake. A pattern is evidence."

I took a breath. Then another. I needed more. I needed to find every discrepancy, build a complete case, and understand the full scope before I did anything with this information.

Because if I was right, Tyler had committed a crime. A federal crime. And Margaret had let him. Another chill ran through me. This one felt different. Not fear. Something else. Something cold, focused, and deadly.

I'd spent months learning his business, understanding his moves, and watching him fail. Now I'd found something he'd tried to hide. Something that could destroy him.

My chest felt tight, but in a good way. Like waking up after years of sleep. I saved the spreadsheet, closed my laptop, and went to check on Grace.

She was building a tower with blocks, knocking it down, laughing, and trying again.

"Mama! Look!"

"I see you, baby. That's so tall."

She beamed at me and went back to her blocks.

I sat down on the floor next to her. My hands had finally stopped shaking, and my heart rate was slowing back to normal. But something had changed. I could feel it in my bones. I'd found a crack in Tyler's empire. A real one, hidden in footnotes he thought no one would read.

I wasn't going to tell anyone yet. I wasn't going to do anything with it, not until I found more, not until I had everything. But sitting there on the floor watching Grace play, I felt something I hadn't felt in months.

Hope.

Not the naive kind. The cold, calculated kind. The kind that comes from finding your enemy's weakness and knowing exactly where to strike when the time is right.

I picked up one of Grace's blocks and handed it to her. She added it to her tower.

"More, Mama!"

"More," I agreed. More blocks for Grace. More evidence for me.

I'd keep digging, keep learning, keep finding every lie Tyler had buried in those reports.

Grace's tower fell. She laughed and started building again. I watched her and smiled. Patient. Determined. Building something one piece at a time.

Maybe she'd learned that from me after all.

Chapter Ten

The Breaking Point

NINE MONTHS INTO TYLER'S tenure as CEO, he announced Carrington Menswear, a media company launching a clothing line.

By then, I had taken more advanced finance online courses: Advanced Financial Statement Analysis, Corporate Valuation, and Detecting Financial Fraud.

All refreshers. All skills I had learned at Ohio State or in McKinsey training. But the muscle memory was coming back faster now.

I remembered the frameworks, the questions we would ask to find weaknesses, and the red flags we had been trained to spot.

Joe Freyer had been obsessed with fraud detection. We had spent weeks analyzing Enron's collapse, studying exactly how they had hidden debt, how they had inflated revenue, and what the warning signs were.

I had thought I would never use that training again; it turned out I had just been saving it.

The menswear announcement was absurd. I read the press release three times trying to understand the logic: a media company making clothes.

CNBC brought Tyler on for an interview, and the host's skepticism was barely disguised.

"Tyler, help me understand the strategy here. What does Carrington Media know about manufacturing menswear?"

"It's about brand extension. We have incredible reach through our media properties. Why not leverage that into adjacent consumer sectors?"

"But you're a media company. Your expertise is content and advertising, not fashion and retail."

"Steve Jobs didn't know anything about phones before the iPhone." Tyler smiled. "Disruption comes from thinking differently."

"Did you just compare a menswear line to the iPhone?"

The interview got tense after that. Tyler kept pivoting to talking points while the host kept pressing for actual business reasoning.

It ended awkwardly. The stock dropped another five percent. I added it to my spreadsheet and created a new tab: "Bad Decisions."

Jim Cramer had Tyler on Mad Money the next week, and his tone had changed.

"Tyler, I've been following your moves, and I have to be honest, I'm concerned. The StreamMedia acquisition isn't performing. Now you're getting into menswear? Help me understand why shareholders should be confident."

"Jim, respectfully, I think you're looking at individual moves instead of the comprehensive strategy."

"Then help me see the comprehensive strategy. Because right now it looks like you're throwing money at random ideas."

"That's not true. It's a strategic pivot to—"

"Tyler." Cramer leaned forward. "Your stock is down twenty-five percent since you took over. Your debt is up seventy percent. Three senior executives have left. Where's the value creation?"

Tyler's face flushed red. "We're playing the long game. If you can't see past quarterly results—"

"I'm asking about basic business fundamentals, and you're giving me buzzwords."

The interview went viral, not in a good way. Carrington Media dropped to seven billion in market cap, down thirty percent from when Tyler started.

I watched the Mad Money clip five times, not because I enjoyed seeing him squirm, but because I was studying him.

His tells, the way he deflected, and the way his jaw clenched when cornered.

At McKinsey, we'd been trained to read executives. We had an entire workshop: "Executive Body Language and Deception Indicators," taught by a former FBI interrogator.

Micro-expressions. Defensive postures. Voice changes under stress.

At the time, I thought it was corporate theater. Now, I was grateful for it. Tyler was drowning. And lying to cover it.

Grace toddled over while I was watching. "Mama, what you watching?"

"Nothing, baby. Just work stuff."

"Come play!"

I closed the laptop and got down on the floor with her blocks. But my mind was elsewhere. Tyler was cracking. I could see it.

And I couldn't look away.

Twelve months in, Tyler bought Caldwell & Main's department stores for six hundred million dollars.

The press conference was a disaster. Reporters packed the room. The mood was different now: skeptical and aggressive.

"Tyler, your menswear line has been discontinued after losing forty million dollars. Now you're buying department stores? What's the connection?"

"Caldwell & Main's provides flagship retail locations for the Carrington brand experience."

"What Carrington brand experience? You're a media company that lost forty million dollars on a clothing line."

"We're building something bigger than traditional media."

"What you're building is debt. Two point three billion in new debt, to be exact. How do you service that?"

Tyler's face was red now. "These are investments in future growth."

"They look like desperate attempts to justify a position you're not qualified for."

I watched it live. Grace was napping. I sat riveted.

Tyler was visibly angry now, his voice rising. "I don't think you understand—"

"We understand your stock is down forty percent. We understand you've burned through billions on failed acquisitions. We understand executives are fleeing. What we don't understand is why shareholders should trust you."

Tyler stood up. "This press conference is over."

He walked out. The cameras kept rolling. Reporters shouted questions at his back. The stock dropped fifteen percent in one day.

That night, CNBC ran a special: "The Fall of Carrington Media: What Went Wrong?"

They interviewed former executives and industry analysts, all saying the same thing: Tyler Carrington was in over his head.

I watched the whole thing. Grace was asleep. I sat in the dark with my laptop.

One analyst said, "He was handed a ten-billion-dollar company with decades of operational excellence. And in twelve months, he's made a series of decisions that appear designed to destroy value."

Another said, "The board should have never approved this succession plan. Nepotism and competence aren't the same thing."

The documentary ended with Margaret declining to comment.

I thought about her in that conference room two and a half years ago, handing me a check and telling me to disappear.

She'd protected Tyler then. Was she still protecting him now as he destroyed everything she'd built?

News articles started appearing. Not just business coverage, but hit pieces.

"Is Tyler Carrington Destroying His Mother's Legacy?"

"Inside the Toxic Culture at Carrington Media"

Then something interesting happened.

A Bloomberg article quoted "sources close to the board" saying Margaret was "increasingly concerned" about the company's direction.

Then Wall Street Journal: "Margaret Carrington Reportedly Pressuring Board to Intervene"

Then Reuters: "Carrington Media Board Discusses CEO Transition Options"

Margaret was trying to save her company, trying to reverse her decision to put Tyler in charge. But she couldn't just fire him. He was her son. It would destroy the family and admit she'd made a catastrophic mistake.

So she was doing it quietly, leaking to reporters and pressuring the board behind closed doors.

I felt a strange satisfaction reading those articles. Margaret had protected Tyler his whole life, covered up his crimes, and put him in a position he couldn't handle.

Now she was watching him destroy everything she'd built. And she was trapped. She couldn't remove him without admitting she'd enabled him, nor could she leave him in place without losing her legacy.

Perfect.

One executive gave an interview to CNBC a month after leaving: "I couldn't stay in an organization where financial discipline was being compromised for short-term optics."

Financial discipline. Compromised.

That was code. That was him saying what he couldn't say directly. The books were being cooked. I added it to my evidence file.

Grace turned three. Small party. Cake. Presents.

She couldn't blow out the candles. Her motor skills were still too delayed. She clapped while Linda and I blew them out for her.

During present opening, my phone buzzed.

CARRINGTON MEDIA Q3 LOSS EXCEEDS EXPECTATIONS, STOCK DOWN 18%

I pulled it out to read.

Linda's voice was sharp. "It's Grace's birthday."

"I know."

"Then why are you checking that?"

"It's just—"

"An obsession?" Linda crossed her arms. "Do you even know what Grace just opened?"

I looked at my daughter. She was holding a book, looking at me with those big eyes.

"Goodnight Moon, Mama! My favorite!"

The words came out wrong. "Favorite" sounded like "fay-vit." Speech delays that therapy was helping but couldn't fix completely.

"That's wonderful, baby."

I put my phone away, got down on the floor, and read Goodnight Moon three times while Grace signed along with the words she knew. But my mind was elsewhere.

That night, after Grace was asleep, I listened to the recorded analyst call.

Tyler sounded broken. His voice flat. Lifeless.

"We're disappointed in the results. We're implementing restructuring initiatives to improve operational efficiency."

"Tyler, your restructuring has been ongoing for a year. When do we see results?"

Silence. Long enough to be uncomfortable.

"Tyler? Are you there?"

"I'm here." His voice cracked. Actually cracked. "These are complex challenges that require—"

"Tyler, are you okay?"

"I'm fine. Next question."

But he wasn't fine. Anyone could hear it.

An analyst asked about the debt load. Tyler's answer was rambling. Incoherent. Another asked about executive departures. Tyler said, "People who don't share the vision don't belong here."

"How many people have to leave before you realize maybe the vision is the problem?"

"I'm not going to—" Tyler's voice broke. "We need to end this call."

"Tyler, we have twenty minutes left—"

"It's over. Thank you."

The line went dead.

Analysts on social media were stunned. "Did Tyler Carrington just have a breakdown on an earnings call?"

CNBC ran it as breaking news, bringing on psychologists to analyze his mental state.

The stock dropped to $1.8 billion. I sat in the dark, listening to it again and again.

This was it. Tyler was collapsing. The company was collapsing.

And I was the only one who knew just how bad it really was.

Grace came over. "Mama sad?"

"Mama's okay, baby."

But I wasn't okay. I was watching a man destroy himself publicly. The man who raped me.

And I felt... what?

Satisfaction? Yes.

But also something else. Something uncomfortable.

I'd sold my silence for his freedom, let him walk away, and now he was destroying himself anyway. Maybe justice doesn't need our help. Maybe it just takes time. Or maybe I was telling myself that to feel better about taking the money.

I spent the next week working on something different.

Not just tracking Tyler's failures anymore. Building something real. Something I could use.

I had two years of Carrington Media financial data now: quarterly reports, SEC filings, earnings call transcripts, news articles, and industry reports. And I had my McKinsey skills had fully returned. I could see the patterns now and understand what I was looking at.

And what I was looking at was systematic fraud.

Not obvious fraud. Sophisticated fraud. The kind we had studied in the Enron case at McKinsey. The kind CEOs go to prison for.

My hands shook every time I found another piece: revenue recognition pushing sales into the wrong quarters, related-party transactions inflating numbers, off-balance-sheet debt hidden in special purpose vehicles.

Caldwell & Main's losses were being concealed, structured through shell companies, buried in footnotes. Classic Enron playbook.

I worked on it for fifteen days straight, every night after Grace went to sleep, sometimes until 3 AM. My eyes burned, and my back ached from hunching over my laptop, coffee going cold beside me while I chased numbers through pages of financial statements.

Each new finding sent adrenaline through my body, made my pulse race, and made my hands shake so badly I had to stop typing and just breathe.

By the fifteenth day, I had seventy-three pages, every irregularity documented, every suspicious transaction highlighted, and every claim supported by data pulled from public filings. I used the McKinsey template I still had saved, the fraud detection framework we had developed for clients.

This was the kind of analysis that had gotten me promoted at McKinsey, the kind executives paid hundreds of thousands of dollars for. Now it was my weapon.

I saved it: "CMG_Fraud_Analysis_CONFIDENTIAL.p df."

I stared at the file for a long time, my cursor hovering over the name, my chest tight.

Four years ago, this would have been my consulting deliverable. Now it was evidence that Tyler Carrington was committing securities fraud.

I closed my laptop and sat in the dark, my whole body vibrating with something I couldn't name.

I didn't know what to do with it at first.

I couldn't go to the SEC; an anonymous tip from a nobody wouldn't trigger an investigation. I couldn't go to the press; no journalist would take fraud allegations seriously without inside sources.

So I started researching other options, lying in bed at night scrolling through my phone while Grace slept beside me. Short sellers, activist investors, firms that profited from exposing fraud.

I found dozens of examples: companies whose stock prices collapsed after research reports exposed accounting irregularities. Enron. Valeant. Wirecard. Luckin Coffee. The most famous firm was Blackwood Research. They had exposed fifteen fraudulent companies in the last decade and made billions shorting stocks before they collapsed.

My heart started racing just reading about them.

I read everything I could find: how they operated, how they sourced information, their track record, every company they had destroyed.

They had a website with a contact form: "Suspect fraud? Submit evidence here."

I stared at that form for three days. If I sent them my analysis, they might investigate, might publish, might destroy Tyler's company. Or they might ignore it.

Those three days were torture. Grace needed me constantly. Therapy appointments. Meltdowns over clothing textures, hours trying to get her to eat, hours trying to get her to sleep. And the whole time, my phone sat in my pocket with that webpage bookmarked. Waiting.

At night, I'd pull it up, read the submission form, type a sentence, delete it, close the browser, and open it again.

My hands shook every time. My stomach twisted. My mouth went dry. This felt different from just researching or learning. This was crossing a line. Taking action. Sending this report meant declaring war.

On the third night, Grace had a meltdown at bedtime, screaming about her pajamas. The seams bothered her. The tags scratched. Everything was wrong and overwhelming, and she couldn't make it stop.

I held her while she cried. Changed her pajamas three times. Finally found a pair she could tolerate. Rocked her until she exhausted herself to sleep.

She was fighting her disability every single day, never giving up, even when everything was harder for her than it should be. If she could keep fighting, so could I.

I laid her in her crib, kissed her forehead, and went to my room to open my laptop. I pulled up the Blackwood Research submission form, my heart pounding in my ears, my whole body electric with fear, adrenaline, and something else. Something cold and sharp.

Determination, maybe. But I couldn't send it from home. Too traceable. Too risky. I decided to send it the next day anonymously at a library.

For now, I opened my nightstand drawer. The compass was there. Still cracked. Still broken.

What I was about to do... sending that email, exposing Tyler, declaring war... this wasn't the north Dad had meant. This wasn't righteousness or protection or staying pure.

This was revenge. Cold. Calculated. Morally gray at best.

And maybe that was okay. Maybe broken people need a broken compass. Maybe when the world takes everything from you, you stop following someone else's definition of right and start making your own.

I closed the drawer, leaving the compass behind. I was choosing my own direction now, and it led through the fire.

The next morning, I told Linda I needed to run errands. I drove to the library downtown. The big one with public computers and anonymous internet access.

My hands were sweating on the steering wheel the whole drive. My pulse was racing. I felt like I was going to throw up.

I found a computer in the back corner, away from the windows and other people. I created an anonymous email account. Proton mail. Encrypted. Untraceable.

My fingers were shaking so badly that I mistyped the password three times. I logged into the email, opened a new message, and went to the Blackwood Research website on my phone to copy the submission email address.

Pasted it into the "To" field. I sat there staring at the empty message box, my heart hammering against my ribs and a cold sweat breaking out on my back.

This was it. The moment everything changed. Once I sent this, there would be no taking it back. No pretending I was just watching, just learning, just understanding my enemy.

This was an attack. A real one.

I thought about Tyler. About his smug face on those earnings calls, about Margaret protecting him, about the settlement money, about Grace, about everything they'd taken from me.

I attached the PDF and typed a brief message.

"Tyler Carrington is committing securities fraud at Carrington Media Group. Attached is a comprehensive analysis documenting systematic accounting irregularities. All data sourced from public SEC filings. This is real. Someone needs to investigate."

My finger hovered over the send button. One click. That's all it would take.

My whole body was vibrating: heart pounding, mouth dry, that electric feeling running through every nerve.

I clicked send.

The email whooshed away. Gone. Irreversible.

I sat there staring at the "Message Sent" confirmation. My whole body trembled. I had to grip the edge of the desk to steady myself.

What had I just done?

I logged out of everything, cleared the browser history, and stood up on legs that didn't feel steady.

I walked out of the library into bright sunlight that felt too harsh, too real. I got in my car and sat there with my hands on the steering wheel, shaking.

I'd just sent evidence of Tyler's crimes to one of the most powerful short sellers in the world, a firm that destroyed companies for profit. If they investigated, if they published, Tyler's empire would collapse.

And I'd be the one who pulled the trigger. The thought should have scared me, should have made me regret it. But sitting there in my car outside the library, I felt something else instead.

Relief. Cold, sharp, and clean.

I'd finally done something. Finally fought back. After months of just watching, learning, and obsessing, I'd taken real action.

When I drove home, my heart was still racing. But for the first time in years, I felt like I had power.

Not much. Maybe they'd ignore my email. Maybe nothing would happen. But maybe something would. And that possibility, that tiny chance of justice, felt like breathing after being underwater for years.

I pulled into Linda's driveway, turned off the car, and sat there for a moment longer.

Grace would be waiting, ready for lunch, ready for her afternoon therapy, ready to keep fighting her own battles. And now I was fighting mine. I got out of the car and went inside.

I didn't tell Linda what I'd done. I didn't tell anyone. I just fed Grace lunch, took her to therapy, and acted like everything was normal.

But that night, after Grace fell asleep, I lay in bed staring at the ceiling. My heart was still racing, and my body buzzed with adrenaline.

I'd crossed a line and declared war. There was no going back now, and I was ready for whatever came next.

Chapter Eleven

All In

DAYS PASSED. THEN A week. Then two weeks. Nothing happened. Maybe they'd ignored it. Maybe my analysis wasn't credible enough. Maybe I'd risked everything for nothing.

I kept checking my anonymous email account from the library. Empty. I kept refreshing Blackwood's website. Nothing new. I started convincing myself I'd been foolish to think they'd care.

Then, three weeks after I sent the email, my phone buzzed with a Google alert.

BLACKWOOD RESEARCH ANNOUNCES UP-COMING REPORT ON "PROMINENT MEDIA COMPANY"

My heart stopped. Actually stopped. The kitchen went silent except for the ringing in my ears.

I clicked the article and had to read it three times because the words kept swimming.

Blackwood Research announced today they will publish a comprehensive report on an unnamed "prominent media company" within 72 hours. The firm's Managing Partner declined to name the target but said the report will detail "systematic accounting irregularities that shareholders deserve to know about."

I sat down hard on my kitchen floor. Right there. My legs gave out. My phone was still gripped in my hand. They'd done it. They'd investigated. They were going to publish.

Grace toddled over. She put her small hand on my face. "Mama okay?"

"Mama's okay, baby."

But I wasn't okay. Blackwood Research would publish their report in seventy-two hours. Unnamed company. But I knew. I knew it was Carrington Media because I'd given them the evidence.

My mind was racing. Seventy-two hours. Three days before the report went public. Three days before the stock collapsed.

I opened my brokerage app. I looked at my account balance. $3.127 million sitting in the S&P 500 index fund. Safe. Growing slowly. Exactly what Richard, the banker, had recommended.

But I had three days. Three days when I knew something the market didn't. Three days before Tyler's empire burned.

I could short the stock. The thought hit me like electricity. It made my whole body go still.

At McKinsey, we'd studied short selling in the hedge fund case. Borrowing shares. Selling them at the current price. Buying them back cheaper when the price fell. Pocketing the difference.

It was how Blackwood made billions. How they profited from exposing fraud. And I knew fraud was coming. I knew the stock would collapse. I had seventy-two hours to act before the rest of the world found out.

My pulse was racing. I pulled up Carrington Media's stock price. $2.1 billion market cap. Trading at $43 per share.

When Blackwood published, it would fall. Fall hard. Maybe to $10. Maybe to $5. Maybe lower.

I could sell my entire index fund. All $3.127 million. Short Carrington Media stock. And when it collapsed, I could buy back the shares for pennies. Keep the difference.

My hands were sweating. This was adjacent to insider trading. Not technically illegal because I wasn't an insider. But close. Dancing on the edge.

I thought about Tyler. About Margaret. About the settlement money. About Grace. About Linda working herself to exhaustion for $42,000 a year.

I opened the trading screen, selected my S&P 500 index fund, and clicked sell. All of it. Every share. My finger hovered over the confirm button.

I clicked confirm. The order executed. $3,127,483 moved to cash. Sitting there. Waiting.

Then I searched for Carrington Media's ticker symbol, found the option to short sell, and entered the amount: $3 million. Maximum position size.

At $43 per share, that was 69,767 shares.

If the stock fell to $10, I'd make $2.3 million. If it fell to $5, I'd make $2.65 million. If it fell further, even more.

My chest was so tight I couldn't breathe. My whole body was shaking. This was real money. Life-changing money. Made in days from information no one else had.

I clicked confirm. The order executed. I'd just shorted 69,767 shares of Carrington Media at $43. Now I had to wait.

I couldn't sleep for the next three days. I couldn't eat. I could barely focus on Grace. The short position sat in my account like a bomb. Ticking. Waiting to explode.

Linda noticed but didn't ask. Grace needed me constantly, but I was somewhere else. Checking my phone every few minutes. Watching the stock price. Watching time pass.

Tuesday morning, the stock was still at $43. Tuesday afternoon, $42.80. People were nervous. Rumors were spreading about which company Blackwood was targeting.

Tuesday night, I sat on the couch with my laptop and phone. Grace was asleep. Linda was in her room. The apartment was so quiet I could hear my own heartbeat.

11:03 PM.

My phone buzzed.

BREAKING: BLACKWOOD RESEARCH RELEASES EXPLOSIVE REPORT ON CARRINGTON MEDIA

Everything went still. The room. The world. My breath. Time itself seemed to stop.

I opened it with hands that wouldn't stay steady. I started reading. The title alone made my chest tight.

"House of Cards: Systematic Fraud at Carrington Media Group"

Forty-seven pages. I scrolled through them faster and faster. My pulse was racing. My vision was tunneling. Every piece of evidence I'd sent them was there. Plus more. They'd done their own investigation, found additional fraud, interviewed whistleblowers, and subpoenaed documents.

But the framework was mine. The analysis was mine. I could see my work throughout. My spreadsheets. My methodology. My exact wording in places.

They'd used everything I'd given them.

My whole body shook so hard I had to set the phone down, press my palms against my thighs, and breathe. Just breathe.

The report's conclusion hit me like a physical blow:

"Carrington Media Group engaged in systematic securities fraud under Tyler Carrington's leadership. Actual value: approximately $100 million. Down from $10 billion eighteen months ago. We recommend immediate divestment."

One hundred million. From ten billion. Ninety-nine percent gone.

I opened my brokerage app with hands that felt disconnected from my body. I watched the stock price update during after-hours trading.

11:15 PM: $24 (down 44%)11:30 PM: $16.34 (down 62%)11:45 PM: $9.03 (down 79%)12 PM: Trading halted.

I stared at the numbers, did the math in my head, then on my calculator, and then again because it couldn't be right.

I'd shorted at $43. The stock was at $9.

$43 - $9 = $34 profit per share.

69,767 shares × $34 = $2,37 million profit.

Plus, my original $3.1 million.

Total: $5,5 million.

I'd made $2.37 million in one day.

In one day.

The room started spinning. I set my phone down, pressed my hands against my thighs, and tried to breathe.

$2.37 million. In less than twenty-four hours. From a single trade.

Linda made $42,000 a year, before taxes, working full-time at a diner. On her feet all day, dealing with difficult customers and her manager monitoring her every move.

I did the math; I couldn't help it.

$2.37 million ÷ $42,000 = 56.4 years.

I'd just made more money than Linda would make in fifty-six years of working. In one day. From clicking buttons on my phone.

The comparison made me feel sick.

Linda had taken me in when I had nothing, fed me, housed me, and watched Grace while I rebuilt my life. She asked for nothing in return except that I stay sober and be a good mother.

She'd worked every day for four years to keep us afloat, picked up extra shifts, and covered my expenses when I couldn't. Never complained. Never made me feel like a burden. And I'd just made more in one day than she'd make in half a century.

I went to her room and knocked softly. She opened the door in her pajamas, hair in a messy bun, and her face tired.

"You okay?" she asked. "You've been weird all week."

"I need to tell you something."

We sat on her bed, the same bed we'd shared as kids when we were scared of Dad, when we'd made promises to protect each other.

"The settlement money," I said, my voice shaking. "I invested it."

"I know. You put it in that S&P 500 index fund."

"I moved it three days ago. I... I shorted Carrington Media stock."

Linda blinked. "What does that mean?"

"It means I bet that Tyler's company would fail. And it did. The stock collapsed tonight. And I made..." I couldn't say it. I couldn't make the words come out.

"How much?"

"$2.37 million. In one day."

The silence was deafening.

Linda just stared at me, her face completely blank, like she couldn't process what I'd said.

"Say that again."

"I made $2.37 million today. From one trade. I have $5.5 million in my account now."

Linda stood up, walked to her window, and looked out at the dark street. Her shoulders were rigid.

"That's more than I'll make in my entire life," she said quietly. "Even if I work until I'm eighty. Even if I never spend a penny."

"I know."

"You made it in one day."

"I know."

She turned around. Her face was hard to read. Not an-gry. Something else.

"How?"

"I found evidence that Tyler was committing fraud. I sent it to Blackwood Research. They investigated and published a report tonight. The stock collapsed. I knew it was coming, so I shorted it."

"Is that legal?"

"Technically, yes. I'm not an insider. But it's based on the research I did using publicly available info..." I trailed off. "So, it's not insider info, and it's legal..."

Linda sat back down on the bed and put her head in her hands.

"I work sixty hours some weeks," she said, her voice muffled. "I pick up shifts on weekends. I skip lunch to save money. I buy generic everything. I haven't had a vacation in six years. And you just made more than I'll ever see in my lifetime."

The words hit like punches.

"I know. I know it's not fair. I know—"

"It's not about fair, Olivia." She looked up, her eyes wet. "It's about... I don't even know what it's about. I'm happy for you. I am. You deserve it after everything. But also..."

She wiped her eyes. "Also, it makes me realize how messed up the whole system is. That someone can work their whole life and never have what you made today. That money makes money. That the rich get richer while the rest of us just... work."

I didn't know what to say. She was right. About all of it. I went back to my room, sat on my bed, and stared at my phone showing $5.5 million in my account.

More money than I'd ever imagined having. Made in a single day. From destroying the man who raped me.

Grace made a sound from her crib. I went to her. She was still asleep, thumb in her mouth, face peaceful.

I'd made $2.37 million today. More than most people made in a lifetime. And she had no idea. No idea her mother had just become wealthy from revenge.

I stood there watching her breathe, thinking about Linda in the next room, about the look on her face when I told her, about how money didn't make anything fair. Didn't erase anything. Just showed you more clearly how broken everything was.

I went back to my laptop and opened it. The settlement money sat in my brokerage account, now $5.5 million. Tyler's blood money. Earned by my silence. Multiplied by his destruction.

I opened a spreadsheet and started analyzing. Because this was what I did when the world fell apart. I built models. I analyzed. I found the truth in the numbers.

This was what I'd been trained for at McKinsey: taking a disaster and finding the value underneath.

Current situation: panic-selling at $100 million.

My hands moved across the keyboard, muscle memory. The shaking stopped when I started typing, calculating, and seeing the patterns.

Strip away the fraud. Look at the core business: local news stations that still generated cash, radio networks with real revenue, and traditional media that worked despite Tyler's incompetence. Write off the bad acquisitions, restructure the debt, fire Tyler, and install competent management.

What would it be worth then?

I ran three different valuation approaches. The same methods I'd used in dozens of McKinsey cases: discounted cash flow, comparable companies, and precedent transactions. Every method said the same conclusion.

My estimate: $600-750 million.

The market was panic-selling it down to $100 million. That was an eighty to eighty-five percent discount from its real value.

I sat back and stared at the numbers on my screen. My heart was pounding, not from fear but from possibility.

I checked my brokerage account again: $5.5 million. I started calculating, my hands steady now and my mind clear. At a $100 million valuation, $5 million would buy 5% ownership.

But what if I borrowed more?

My pulse raced. I could borrow against my account and take a securities-backed loan. Banks did this all the time for wealthy clients, and I was a wealthy client now.

$10 million total: $5.5 million from my account and $5 million borrowed.

$10 million at a $100 million valuation equaled 10% ownership.

10% of a company actually worth $600-700 million. 10% that could be worth $60-70 million when it recovered.

The numbers made my chest tight and made it hard to breathe.

But this wasn't about the money. I knew that even as I calculated the returns and modeled the upside. It was about power.

10% meant real voting rights, board representation, and a significant voice in every decision.

Tyler had paid me $2 million to be powerless, to disappear, and to stay silent about what he'd done to me.

Margaret had paid me to give up any claim to their empire, to ensure Grace never touched a penny of their fortune.

Now I could buy my way back in, with their own money, multiplied by their destruction. I could own 10% of Tyler's company, vote on his future, help remove him, and watch him answer to me.

The irony was so beautiful it hurt.

I waited until morning to call Richard, the banker who'd helped me invest the settlement money originally.

"Ms. Parker." His voice was cautious. "I saw the news about Carrington Media. Quite the collapse."

"I need a securities-backed loan: five million dollars against my account."

Silence on the line, long and heavy.

"For what purpose?"

"Investment opportunity: a media company."

Another pause, even longer.

"You're talking about Carrington Media."

"Yes."

"Ms. Parker." His voice was very careful. "That company is collapsing. The fraud report suggests it's worth perhaps one-tenth of its current trading value. The stock is down seventy-nine percent. I cannot in good conscience—"

"I worked at McKinsey in corporate strategy and valuation. I've analyzed this company for two years. Let me walk you through the math."

"I'm listening, but I'm very skeptical."

I explained the core business, the cash flow, the real assets, the stripped-down valuation, the eighty-five percent discount, and the recovery potential.

My voice was steady, my analysis clear. This was what I'd been trained for. This was what I was good at.

"That's... actually compelling analysis," he said finally. "But Ms. Parker, if you're wrong, you lose everything: your settlement money, your daughter's future, everything you've built."

"I know."

"Why take this risk?"

I looked at Grace's bedroom door, at my daughter sleeping behind it.

"Because Tyler Carrington took everything from me. And I'm taking something back."

There was a long silence. I could hear him breathing, thinking.

"I'll structure the loan," Richard said finally. "But you need to understand the terms. This is a high-risk securities-backed loan on an extremely volatile asset. I'm requiring an LLC for asset protection and anonymity. That's non-negotiable."

"I understand."

"And there's something else." His voice became very serious. "If the stock drops more than fifty percent from your purchase price, the bank will issue a margin call. You'll have twenty-four hours to deposit additional funds to cover the loss. If you can't, we will sell your position immediately, without your consent, without discussion. Do you understand?"

My stomach dropped. "If it drops fifty percent—"

"We liquidate your entire position automatically. You lose the investment, and you still owe the five-million-dollar loan. Your account, your settlement money, and everything you made will be used to pay it back. You could lose everything."

"I understand the risk."

"Do you? Ms. Parker, if this stock continues to fall and it's already down seventy-nine percent, you could be wiped out within days. Hours, even. There's no protection, no second chances. The margin call is automatic. You're betting ten million dollars on a company that just lost ninety-nine percent of its value."

I closed my eyes, saw Grace's face, her struggles, her determination, her trust in me to keep her safe.

"I understand."

Another long pause. I could hear papers rustling, him typing.

"All right. I'll structure the deal. God help us both."

"Thank you, Richard."

"Ms. Parker? I hope you're right. Because if you're wrong, there's no coming back from this. You'll lose five and a half million dollars. Everything."

"I know."

Richard was quiet for a long time.

"All right. I'll have the documents ready tomorrow morning. But Ms. Parker? Don't tell your daughter I helped you with this. If it goes wrong, I don't want her to know."

The LLC documents came the next day. I'd chosen the name the night before, sitting in the dark, reflecting on promises, justice, and iron-hard determination.

Iron Justice Holdings LLC

Not Grace's name. Not mine. Nothing that could trace back to us.

But a promise. That justice would come. That it would be hard and unbreakable. That Tyler and Margaret would face consequences for what they'd done. Even if it took years. Even if I had to hide behind corporate structures and anonymous filings.

The name felt right. Like a weapon I was forging in secret. I signed the documents and sent them back. I couldn't breathe.

The stock hit $95 million by Friday morning. My broker executed the purchase that afternoon.

10.2% of Carrington Media Group.

Cost: $10.5 million. My $5.5 million plus the $5 million loan.

The confirmation email came at 3:47 PM. I was sitting on the kitchen floor with Grace. She was playing with blocks, trying to stack them, falling, trying again. Her face was red with effort. Her determination visible in every movement.

My phone buzzed.

Purchase Complete: Iron Justice Holdings LLC - 10. 2% Ownership - Carrington Media Group

I stared at it, read it three times. My vision went blurry.

10.2%. I owned more than 10% of my rapist's company.

"Mama on floor?" Grace looked at me, her face concerned.

"Yeah, baby. Mama's on the floor."

She climbed onto my lap. I held her tight. Her warmth, her weight, her complete trust.

I'd just risked everything: the safety I'd bought with silence, the money meant for Grace's future, the fortune I'd made from Tyler's destruction. All of it tied to a company on the verge of complete collapse.

If the stock dropped another 50%, we'd lose everything. The margin call would trigger. Forced liquidation. Five and a half million gone. Bankruptcy. Ruin.

Either this was the smartest move I'd ever made, or I'd just destroyed us both.

Grace fell asleep in my arms, exhausted from playing, from trying so hard to do simple things her brain and body made difficult.

I sat there holding her, staring at my phone. The confirmation email glowing.

Iron Justice Holdings LLC - 10.2% Ownership

I owned 10% of my rapist's company. Tyler had no idea. Margaret had no idea. The board had no idea.

The woman they'd paid to disappear had just bought a major piece of their empire. With their own blood money.

I started laughing, then crying, then both. I couldn't stop. I couldn't control it. Grace stirred but didn't wake. The laughter turned into sobs. Deep, shaking sobs that came from somewhere I'd kept locked away for years.

I'd done it. I'd actually done it. Crossed every line. Risked everything. Bet our entire future on destroying the people who'd destroyed me. And now I owned 10% of Carrington Media Group. 10% meant real power, real votes. A seat at the table when they discussed Tyler's future.

For the first time in three years, I wasn't just surviving. I wasn't just watching. I was fighting back.

I whispered to Grace in the darkness, "I sold my voice once to keep you safe. Now I'm buying it back. With their money. With their destruction. Watch what happens next."

After she settled deeper into sleep, I returned to my room and opened my nightstand drawer.

The compass sat there, cracked glass. Broken since the day I bought vodka at Murphy's Tavern and found it in Dad's nightstand.

I picked it up. The brass was cold, then warm under my thumb. The needle had been spinning for years, searching. Never settling. Lost, just as I had been.

But now it moved, steadied, and found its direction.

North.

Not because the compass was fixed; the glass was still cracked, the fracture still splitting the face in two.

But I was different now. I wasn't confused anymore. I wasn't questioning what was right or wrong or moral or just. I'd chosen my direction.

My north. Power. Fighting back.

Using their blood money as a weapon.

Iron Justice.

Chapter Twelve

Author's Note

THANK YOU FOR READING ***Book 3 Blood Money***.

I know how Book 3 ends. Olivia just made a choice that will change everything and I'm not going to make you wait to see what happens next.

Book 4: Where Leo Died picks up exactly where we left off. The margin call. The warehouse. The bleeding man on her doorstep. And the moment Olivia has to decide: Grace or justice. She can't have both.

This is the book where everything Olivia's been fighting for collides with everything she's trying to protect. It's raw, it's brutal, and it answers questions you've been asking since Book 1.

Start reading Book 4 by searching "***Where Leo Died by Howard Kane***" wherever you buy books.

A quick favor: If this story has meant something to you, if Olivia's struggle, Grace's resilience, or the messy reality of recovery and revenge resonated, would you leave a short review on wherever you buy books? Even 2-3 sentences help other readers find these books. It makes a real difference.

Book 4: *Where Leo Died* is waiting. Don't make Olivia wait alone in that warehouse.

Thank you for reading.

With gratitude,

Howard Kane

264

This page was intentionally left blank.

This page was intentionally left blank.

This page was intentionally left blank.

This page was intentionally left blank.